# Spying on the MONSTERS' FESTIVAL

I0677811

## Auxie Mzil-Lehang

Spying on the Monsters' Festival

Written by Auxie Mzil-Lehang

Published by Hoart Benom (Pty) Ltd - Publishing

Cape Town, South Africa

To order books or for customer service, please email

oxy.lehang@gmail.com

ISBN 978-0-620-91378-2

This book is printed on acid-free paper ∞

★ ★ ★

*To McNaughton, my husband, I fail to find the perfect words –
but thank you for always being there and allowing me to beat
the drum to my own rhythm. You took the hit and heat; writing
burns, it's hard work!!*

*My son CML Chris, this is for you!*

*Everisto, Agatha, Tracy and Nashel – love you always...*

*To my parents, Blazio and Beauty – I'm forever indebted. Pa, I
get this from you. You're such a great storyteller and teacher.
You introduced me to the art of putting words together at a
very young age; I fell in love and haven't stopped scribbling.*

*To all my friends and fans – tons of love.*

TERAS

# I

*Ka-boom!*
I give a bow,
Gossip time – oh, yes gossip.
It's that time of the year once again.
I've finally discovered a great deal – all that unfolds
on the big day; dawn to dusk, precisely...
'GOTHIC!'

The usually bustling city centre of the Arcane Capital looked unquestionably deserted. It was the day of the Monsters' Festival. Most shops and other outlets had begun winding up four days previously, in preparation for the closure. They were very certain that chaos was bound to befall on the fateful day and the whirl would most likely bubble over, cascading to undesignated areas of the closest neighbouring lands.

It was a very special day for monsters in the nearby kingdom, Colossus, when they got together in honour of their remarkable tradition.

It happened over and over; they behaved like they had just signed a deed of conveyance to possess that entire part of the world every time they held the huge fiesta. Nothing else ever mattered to them except achieving their own maximum *gemütlichkeit.* They held the lavish celebrations once yearly. It had been felicitously christened and known as *Colossus Monsters' Boisterous Day*!

The burly-built, six-armed giant Jack-eyed, who was the reigning king of Colossus, was the first one to arrive at the venue on the day. As the leader, he was also to be the master of ceremonies according to their tradition. The festival was to be held at the prestigious Behemoth Hall.

It was very early, nautical dawn, when the Monster-king got to Behemoth. He took a couple of slow, deep breaths, puffing his chest – in and out, in and out – feeling the intimate flow of air. His exhalation gusted out into the crisp atmosphere like scalding steam swirling from the spout of a hot teapot.

As soon as he entered the gate, he leaned back against a boulder and took a prolonged pause to meditate. There was a whiff of earth coming from organic debris, combined with a fresh green scent that rose with no interruptions from the surrounding trees and other plants. Untarnished nature. He could not resist marvelling at the gushy scent, as it was gently transported into his space by the early morning wind. To him, it depicted the warm promise of a successful Boisterous Fiesta. It got him utterly enthusiastic and he exuded infectious confidence. With broadened shoulders and flamed-up chest, he was ready for the next item on the Boisterous Day To Do list – security checks. Behemoth gate had still not been fixed after the top hinge had been ripped off in a barbaric wild rush that had sprung up on the day of the previous fiesta. The top structure of the gate had been apparently left deformed too.

Without delay, Jack-eyed embarked on the essential operation... going right around Behemoth yard, carefully scanning every angle, hunting down anything awry. He trampled on a thick carpet of fallen leaves and branches. His feet went stumping all the way around, with every step making a very loud rustling noise, which echoed in the nearby shrubby thicket. Nobody ever raked away the dead matter. It belonged.

Jack-eyed's orbs kept sharply alert as he manoeuvred around, slowly performing his tasks. Right off the bat, a shiny object caught his eye. He was now at the middle section at the back of the building. It was a tin; lodged behind a gutter, adjacent to where he stood still. He glared at it with a quizzical expression on his face. It was metallic – light refractive, and yellowish in colour. The object was more or less the size of a large ostrich egg, but perfectly cylindrical and corrugated. They never used or touched such a thing. Not in Colossus. If the mammoth leader's eyes spat fire, in nanoseconds the tin would incinerate. He fought with it with his glare...

Later on, he picked up a long stick from close by and broke it in half for easier grip. He used the other piece to push out the metal tin from behind the gutter. It was not difficult at all; it rolled out to the open in just a bit, and his eyes rolled together with it. He lifted his massive foot up, exerting a great amount of energy, and crushed it at once! It went flat right away with a bang. It was empty. After a short respite he hoofed it in anger, but it did not go far. He went after it, picked it up and cast it away with force. To him, the object was trash and he had deemed it to pose danger. It flew over a range of trees and landed by the roadside, in the main street. He clucked. All was fine with him now – as long as it wasn't in the vicinity of Behemoth.

The quest had to go on...

The place was dead quiet, except for constant sounds that came from croaking frogs, chirping crickets and other wild creatures. Nobody ever trespassed into Behemoth centre; that was absolutely out of the question. Only invisible aliens took chances and intruded!

Although the old structure of the Behemoth building looked strong enough to shelter a multitude of monsters, the outer side of the large concrete building was badly soiled. The plastering was chipping in some areas, and the wall contained visible cracks that were so large that no kind of paint would successfully mask them. There were vines and climber plants that vigorously encroached upon the structure too. Their vibrance was a welcome façade, concealing many of the secrets that were lying beneath. Previous climbers that had died, seemingly good years before, still sat in their original spaces, hanging loose off the wall, and only clasped together by the natural webbing of the live climbers. They stayed there, tangled in clusters, and the masses were stretching right around the entire Behemoth wall. Layers of moulds and mildew that had accumulated on them were now overlaid by the vibrant green leaves of the freshly blooming plants. They knitted methodically in-between the dead strings.

A flock of birds also made their home at Behemoth centre. It looked a perfect habitat for them – an oasis... elaborate and sanctified. Older birds left their eggs and brood in the day and always found them intact upon return from their foraging for food in different faraway places. At the right time, the young ones were taught how to fly on their own into the skies to start fending for themselves – and it all happened there at Behemoth. Eventually, they built their own nests around the area. It was a cycle.

The presence of the birds, however, trailed along with a nerve-wracking feel of ghostly phantoms hovering all over the space as several nests snuggled around throughout the building – clinging as they did within the pockets of the vampiric plants. The noxious look was toned down slightly by the appearance of scattered bloomy flowers. It was the favourable season for them, luckily, coinciding with Boisterous Day! They were reddish-brown, displaying on the upper level of the wall – going up toward the crude tiles of the roof. These tiles resembled tree bark and were cut into rectangular shapes and arranged in an overlaid pattern. The flowers appeared on all sides of the main building.

Butterflies also flew on and off quite frequently, and the colourful creatures splashed a tinge of beauty onto the spine-chilling zone.

If proper maintenance work was to be done by the monsters themselves – *oof!* It would be impractical getting it completed in days and, with ordinary human manpower, it would require a good span of months, if not years. As it stood, it was rather proper that it be labelled *Not Suitable for Use* in the human world. Be that as it may, the monstrous owners thought highly of their centre. 'Model of excellence...' was the impression they showed towards Behemoth Hall and their turf as a whole.

Upon having carried out all checks, and with great triumph radiating on his face, King Jack-eyed certified that nothing was out of order. He swaggered back in the direction of the front of the building and proceeded to an adjacent secluded area that was chiefly reserved for ritual purposes. Only high authority ogres were allowed to set foot in the area. He bowed in honour and walked through an arch-shaped arbour, an alleyway that led to the sacred place. In the centre of the arbour perched an unusual object. It was a sculptural design of an adult condor vulture. It was made of metal – very eloquently formed, with the bird's wings fully stretched in a soaring position. Although it had turned a bit rusty, the piece of artwork said something essential about how the powerful vulture was regarded.

The primeval bird was of high symbolism to the tribe. They conceived it had supreme divine strength within. With that belief, and keeping it close at heart, they felt it would impart them with spiritual eyes to enable them to see and evade all the invisible horrors that could possibly be preying on them. They trusted that divine guidance also dwelt in them.

There was, for certain, a hatful of attributes stirring them to desire what this bird symbolized on their emblem. That the condors could naturally go for days without eating was to them a sign of endurance, which they envied. They thought endurance was one of the most important traits spearheading survival... being able to go on boldly without fear, heedless of whatever conditions one might be subjected to. This caused them to idolize the vulture even further.

This monster tribe, in their mannerisms, associated themselves very closely with nature. They believed the condor was kin. In their appraisals, they hailed how it contributed enormously to ameliorating the status quo of the ecosystem, and the bird's power in general was a final flourish in their admiration. The ogres robustly considered the vulture as being able to defeat and incite fear almost effortlessly in many other creatures in the wild. Dreaming of themselves drowning in vulnerability was agony. Soaring was what they believed in – wanted to live for – and to maintain in their world.

# 2

In no time at all, Monster Jack-eyed was done with the invocation rituals. He walked, hunched and staid, all the way from the shrine till out of the arbour. He went forth to unlock and open the Behemoth Hall doors.

The Colossus king just could not resist humming their characteristic Boisterous tune, *Monster Fear*.

The two entrance doors were opened wide, paving the way to welcome the anticipated congregation. Inside the large building were a few compartments reserved for other purposes: including a dedicated kitchen. The hall section was the largest. Weirdly, the hall contained no windows. It only had a few air vents that were set at the level of the trusses. They were also slightly blocked by the climber plants growing on the outside wall. The air vents looked really small in comparison to the monsters' bodily structures – although perhaps anything was bound to seem so when compared to a mammoth. In total, there were only four of these vents, serving the entire sitting area. They used the air vents as spyholes too.

With no windows in place, the inside of the hall was very dark. Natural light was restricted from shining in. The walls were primarily painted in a bush green colour, with a few distinct areas that were adorned with mustard yellow. It was the green of lively dark leaves on the trees and the yellow of them before detaching from the mother tree. It probably signified the natural change of things in general.

Funnily, the main entrance of the hall looked absolutely phenomenal and thrilling. It was beautified by large artworks that were engraved right across on the wall. The theme was aggressively baroque, as was befitting the mystical culture of mammoths. The works of art lay behind the platform, and it was obligatory to respect that area. It was like a kind of museum, with candid decorations of animal horns and beaded astragals. However, they did not have to kill animals for the purpose. They exclusively utilized the remains of powerful creatures upon their natural death.

Numerous grooved curly horns were attractively aligned horizontally, forming two decorative parallel lines for an outer border. The horns were short, and the curly ends brought about a spectacular radiant design as they slightly interlocked at every connective joint. Very long and thin horns – likely that of Scimitar antelope – were embedded inside the border, protruding outwards. They were roughly a metre long and looked evocatively as though they were still alive, implanted on their biological host. A couple of other horns, closely resembling dry tree branches, were randomly laid inside the border, and right in the centre of the piece was a mounted head of a fully-grown lion. The large cat was quite frightening, with the mouth wide open, exposing its formidable teeth as if it were set to pounce! Clustered beads and chatoyant stones added extra charm to the wall. The whole thing showed the utmost skill and it was authentic avant-garde art – simply unforgettable.

# 3

It never took long before Monster Johnny-Warlock flourished. It was shortly after King Jack-eyed formally opened up. The two were relatively close pals. Warlock helped out with the lighting up of candles, and they arranged them around the hall in a straight path against the wall. The large room was filled with the warmth of many yellow flames. Although they were tiny, the flames flickered bright through numerous perforations of wooden shades, under which the candles had been placed. The shades were of medium height – hexagonal in shape, and open on either end. On the extreme edges of the hexagonal wooden structures were little *gidee-gidee* peas stuck all around, with their eyes facing the front. They came up with their own creations and designed most of them themselves, there in Colossus – start to finish.

Immediately after greetings and candle lighting, the long-shanked monster Johnny-Warlock ambled back to Behemoth entryway. He slouched by the wrecked gate and patiently waited for fellow monsters to arrive. He busied himself scratching his body. Johnny-Warlock's body was partially covered with scales that lay arranged in a natural pattern. At times, the scales flaked, causing itchiness. It was his life. He was used to the routine. All mimsy in the cool breeze, he scoured and scored – unrestrained whilst in the waiting.

The hours were still very young and mosquitoes were candidly very active at work. A large scourge whined all around the area, but it was no big deal to Johnny-Warlock. He just sat there quietly. He neither snapped nor tried to swat any of the blood-sucking insects away. The monster was not even up to changing his sitting spot either. It seemed rather melodic and amusing to him. As comfortable as he looked, with his face elated, Johnny-Warlock squinched one eye and the mosquitoes went abuzz and *gaga* – sucking the red liquid from his body for survival. The tiny insects bred freely in the peat bog that was right next to the gate, inside the yard. But biding his time waiting for folks was paramount.

Junior monsters forming the chefs' brigade arrived. It was quite a large number of selected individuals. They headed straight to Behemoth kitchen. The kitchen door was already flung open. It could only be unlocked from inside. Their monster head cook was scurrying right behind them. They put on their aprons and promptly started with the food preparations. There were absolutely no minutes left aside to spare.

Johnny-Warlock made sure he hand-shook or patted every monster on the back, as they arrived. "Happy Boisterous Day!" he exclaimed as he greeted fellow kinsmen. Every monster looked zippy and zealous. They all looked forward to a delightful festival. "I want a kiss on the cheek," said Monster-Monsleek, pointing a finger to her right cheek. She closed her eyes, stretching herself on toes like a danseuse to reach Johnny-Warlock's height.

"*Bahahaha...* I see you ogress – your colourful disposition at play!" He went on to give her pecks on both of her cheeks. She was chuffed. "Be good today..." Johnny called out from behind her back, and she waved back, cackling.

King Jack-eyed's best companion, Monster Fiery-Fireball, also arrived early for the first time in many years. The grey-furred mammoth Fiery-Fireball was already shouting meaningless points of correction to others, which brought about unnecessary confusion in the very early hours of the festival day. He was clumsily up and down. One minute he was in the hall and in the next, in the kitchen and in the following, loitering outside. Most monsters wished that the ogre had arrived much later or had even failed to show up. They openly complained about how obnoxious he was.

Whenever there was trouble, Fiery-Fireball would be present; not as a spectator but to heighten the state of affairs. "Mess with me and I'll throw my fireballs right into your face!" Fiery-Fireball always threatened his fellows. He was boastful of the pellets that he crafted. He was the only ogre that knew how to make them, and he kept his lips sealed about the process. The pellets exploded out of their sheaths, emitting heat and flashes of light upon striking onto surfaces. The king would not say much;

he thought it would ruin the budding type of friendship they shared, and the shots did not cause serious harm, apparently. Fiery-Fireball also gave a hand sometimes, to help punish those found on the wrong side of principles.

Most feared and repulsive Twelve-eyed Monster obviously came, and was punctual. He held a highly respected position within the tribe. He was already taking down points to note and would give a review later on in the day. The famous hyper-active Monster-Monsleek was now mingling in the huge crowd with fellow monsters. Her behavioural attributes made folks laugh most of the time, and she also loved cracking jokes. Being the cynosure of all eyes was what she craved the most. The bubbly ogress's alluring light-heartedness struck a chord with many; they would easily get very comfortable in her presence. Her conduct was however disputable sometimes, as she too was capable of causing a commotion at festivals, especially after getting drunk, although it was seldom that happened.

"Did you notice the big patch on Fiery-Fireball's neck...?" Monster-Monsleek had already started. She laughed up her sleeve, gossiping with Avid-Thwack, another female monster, a companion within her ring of friends.

"Hey, it's bald; that I saw! One of his meteor pellets most probably backfired – and that one must've been a spectacular bash! Just look at the blemish again, *I mean...*" Avid-Thwack responded chuckling and had everyone else in stitches. Fiery-Fireball was oblivious of what was going on behind his back.

"No wonder he never told me about it, I suppose," she remarked. "We normally share everything," she went on, thrusting cursory glances at Fiery-Fireball.

Her upper jaw teeth, the middle canines, were grossly large and sharp at the tip. The teeth stood out like intimidating weapons. They encroached on her chin. Avid-Thwack had pride in these teeth. They were useful for scything meat, and not many had such endowment.

# 4

The very first hiccup on the epic day bobbed up when the invited guests from Teras Kingdom arrived. Monster-Jumbo could not fit in through the door. Doors wide open, main entrance, and everyone else going through; it just did not work out for Jumbo. With all he had invested, planning for the big day, and the egoism of representing his own kingdom, he had to get in. He was proudly wearing an orange T-shirt, that was popping the name **TERAS**, written in bold black. He was geared up for the day, but his body was four times bulkier than most of the congregants. He was the largest of all, with an elephantine foot-size. Jumbo might have underestimated how much more he had grown since he'd last stepped into the famous Behemoth centre, a couple of years back.

Hunkering would cram his muscles into bulges, which would still prevent him easily getting through. He still tried though! It was with no success. But, the giant of the giants was stubborn. His peers also stood by him, observing and pepping him up.

After a brief, thoughtful moment Jumbo remarked, "You've made really big changes to your doorway I see - it's literally more of a toehole now." His analogy was however received as jape, which invoked a clutter of guffaws.

He ambled backwards... about twelve steps. Other monsters simply made way for him. What he was up to, they were yet to discover. They kept following his movements closely. His arms were dangling as if some nerves had gone lifeless. Suddenly, he stopped. The ogre growled; pumping up force - an effort that was mimicked by the woods with deafening echoes. He ran headlong, straight at the entryway. He got stuck! Once again, he'd notched up yet another flopped strategy. Only part of his arms crossed over, but under no circumstances would he or any other folk from Teras waste their special invite. He was eager to keep trying.

"Team work - team work, let's be worker bees for a *sec*! Jumbo, why don't you run in, I mean give it another shot? We'll all push you from behind - lest we're all scrapped out for the first course," Monster-Monsleek proposed, crackling the dry leaves as she waltzed right from the back of the crowd. Her chest was puffed up. "Food-Killer and her team always have a wild mind of their own," Monsleek lamented. She was flexing her wrists as if she were ever in a position to render any effort of significance. The vivacious female monster had been trapped outside, together with her circle of friends, where they were relishing their coveted game of gossiping.

"I'll do it myself, Colossus Queen, please don't be bothered – won't be a *forever and a day mission*. Nonetheless, thanks," Jumbo quickly responded, before she spiralled out of hand.

"Perfect one! Then wrap it up oh, please. It's torment sighting the gateway to Shangri-La barricaded like this," she whined.

Monsleek was short-tempered; she got hacked off too easily. Her personality was very complex, just like the majority of monsters in the tribe. She lowered her chin towards her shoulder and walked away softly like an acrobat. The light wind blew her skirt gently, making the fringes twirl in a very charming manner. It drew attention. The tiny brown beads drifted high up at free will, clinging onto the fringes. Monsleek soaked in the admiration of so many monsters. They kept staring at the foxy ogress as she headed back to where her friends were standing.

There was nothing that would hypnotize Monster-Jumbo, distracting him from fighting his battle. He kept his nose to the grind stone. The male mammoth threw himself onto the ground. He then tried crawling in like a human baby. There was no turning back for him. *One...two...one...two* – on his knees he went. It looked positive, easy go initially, then suddenly he got wedged. Again. The body protested! It was at that point that many would surrender. The hulky mammal found it agonising when he stood up, and he realized all the depressions his knees and fists had engraved onto the ground. All bootless effort. In the scuffle, he had cleared up all the debris of fallen leaves and grass that had accumulated over a very long time. In addition to the worms and termites that got exposed, the clearing of the matter caused an intense organic scent of earth, which resonated very well with everybody there. They gushed about it, but it would not work as a pacifier to stretch their patience any longer.

Before trying other techniques, Jumbo had to give way and let all the monsters who had queued behind, also itching to enter, in. They were running amok – exhausted from being spectators of Jumbo's personal hustle to take part in the jubilations. Monster-Monsleek and her crew took the opportunity and went in too.

Just when the Colossus leaders had cordially agreed to resort to breaking down the door and tearing apart its surrounding wall to help their respected guest get in, the Teras giant thought he would give it one more final try. He was not prepared to let his kindred down or embarrass himself by quickly agreeing to such a huge step. He stayed cool.

Confidently taking off his top garments – a chequered jacket that he rolled up, and the T-shirt – Monster-Jumbo threw himself onto the ground again. He laid his body into a mermaid position – face down, with hands straight above his head, and moved in slowly, writhing like a young caterpillar. He slowly but surely hauled his astronomic being from earth onto the hard-concrete floor inside of Behemoth Hall. *Voila!*

Finally, Jumbo managed to thrust his body through. In entirely solid state, he bumbled about, finding the best place to sit. He was all exhausted, but the bliss of just being inside together with everyone else shone in his eyes. His pieces of clothing were back on his body in no seconds. However, there was something wrong with the T-shirt. It looked tighter than before. It would not make sense to speculate that he had gained some more weight in the struggle of getting in – in just a matter of minutes; approximately an hour. His exertions would have rather cost him calories instead. His jacket was open in the front, leaving the entire front part exposed. The T-shirt was really tight – fitting snugly around the neck and chest area.

Checking closely, the letters **T E R A S** were not aligned anymore! They ran diagonally, and some letters were appallingly stretched out – with the 'S' thrown right at the bottom!

Jumbo had worn his T-shirt wrongly – featuring a completely new style.

He wore the armhole part over his head and an arm through the neckline! He had not realised his mistake, or he simply did not care anymore. He had wrestled and accomplished a vital challenge; far more important than anything else.

He sat comfortably, schmoozing effusively amongst everyone else in the hall. Only the orange T-shirt – disorientated as it was – and driblets of sweat on his face bore witness to the struggle.

"Look at you, Jumbo; just look at you!"

"Yes, yes, sure Monsleek, I know! I made it – finally. Yeah, see, I told you."

Monster-Monsleek had turned up out of the blue, exclaiming with awe – although about what exactly was vague. She could have been referring to the giant finally making it inside, or the utterances may simply have referred to the now polo-neck Tee...

Jumbo glowed with his story of success! He was not geared to waste any opportunity for discussion of his accomplishments, or acknowledgment of any praise directed to him.

His brawny hands and knees had saved his day. It was a huge relief too, to Colossus dwellers, that their building had not crumbled down after the numerous shockwaves triggered by the Teras giant's entry endeavours.

# 5

"**N**o time to cut! Just tear the cabbage, stupid! Tsk-tsk you love wasting time... knives to the bin now – I said all the... hey! It's Boisterous *dash*!" The monster head cook was belligerent in the space-constricted kitchen of Behemoth.

"What did I say? Even that onion doesn't need a knife – conscience – conscience... won't it whisper some sense into you? Nature already slits it for you – just peel, dismantle and chuck!"

She blinked nonstop and rested her fists on a table for support... trying to calm her breathing that had gone wayward hyper.

After about a minute, she walked over and picked a few roots from a basket. She stuffed them into her mouth in a flash.

"I hope they're washed," the cuisine master recited in an adenoidal pitch, looking up for a response whilst crunching down the roots. No one answered.

"I see my voice going croaky before the clock even strikes twelve..." Food-Killer complained, making loud breathy noises again. She doddered away from the hub of activity, shaking her head. She explored around for a perfect spot to sit.

She planted herself on a large stockpot, *who cared about what was inside?* The lid protected the contents, although it was dingy with only a few isolated flecks revealing its original colour. Stuck and comfortable on the stockpot, she kept barking orders as she picked her nose. Her eyes, meanwhile, kept wandering unfalteringly, literally turning what is usually a reflex to a free-will action and barely blinking at all.

"Throw me four roots there. I want devil's claws," she called out to a cook who was walking past the basket and they were tossed to her right away. Food-Killer's hands were already open to strike a catch, but they all fell onto the floor just close-by. To the surprise of the cooks who were following, she quietly picked the roots up without any complaints.

She luxuriously extended her legs, resting her feet on a medium-sized cask that was holding extra juice as she crunched down her snack. Despite the day being one of the most scorching summer days, over her rounded fleshy shoulders was a heavy cloak. The heat was also intensified by the high temperatures being generated in the cramped kitchen. It all did not matter to her or anyone else there. The woolly cloak, brown in colour with black patches, meant a lot to Food-Killer. On its lower back part was a hole to allow her pudgy tail to move freely with no obstructions.

The clattering of utensils was very intense, and the monster-cooks were bumping into each other like headless chickens. It was toilsome, back-breaking work but they kept at it. Fire had been put up outside too, to cater for larger drums and a couple of cauldrons.

It was good that beverages were already done and ready. They were all contained in large barrels. Beer had been made a week earlier, and berries juice had been extracted three days before. The juice was a combination of different kinds of berries and wild cherries. The cooks had had an extra job, having had to deseed the bags of cherries first. They'd then crushed all the fruits manually with their hands, passing the juice through large strainers. They simply wore plastic aprons and gloves, then got busy – clobbering and grinding, sucking out as much liquid from the fruits as possible. To do everything on Boisterous Day itself would have been unfeasible. Time was limited.

Making the beer ahead of time also allowed it an opportunity to ferment and reach a specific mature flavour the older ogres treasured. No youngster touched the drink; it was taboo! They were considered still wet behind the ears. For any younger monster to be finally considered a fully-fledged adult ogre they would have only grown one size larger than the averagely built adult human being of about 167 centimetres. To be called an adult ogre, half a size less was still acceptable though, but only singled out monsters at the fully-fledged, senior level handled anything to do with beer – from preparations to the service of it on the very significant day. As for the kitchen brigade, that was also a burden off their shoulders.

On the big day, time was ticking for the cooks. First priority was working on the principal course, protein. No innocent animal was mangled to take care of their most respected dish. Dead animals and birds had been collected in the previous days. The huge task was undertaken by monsters who had volunteered to go searching in faraway mountains. There were not sufficient supplies in the immediate proximity.

The collected lot was massed on the floor – going up on one side of the storeroom. The animals were consuming the better part of the space in the room, making it feel much smaller. They were taken outside at intervals, one batch at a time, to be skinned and have their insides removed for cooking preps.

The cooks started off by working on the beasts' carcasses. It was a very quick and rough chopping job with hatchets. Immediately after, the meat was put to boil in a huge drum. The outside of the drum was filthy and badly scraped. '*...but who would fuss over it*?' To them, all that mattered was getting the meat cooked on time. A splash of water inside of the drum had been sufficient! Not all animal carcasses were put on the heat. Some monsters, the very carnivorous ones – Avid-Thwack and company – preferred it raw. They simply spiced it up and feasted!

As the meat boiled, the monster-cooks concentrated on other things. There were many other tasks at hand. Some worked on fish and snails – whelks, winkles and edible slugs. Others slaughtered frogs, skinning, gutting and dismembering them. Another crew took care of rodents and lizards, and the rest were preparing grain, pumpkins and various leaves and roots.

"Firm on your feet everyone. You fool yourselves if you think that you can be lazy around here!" The monster head cook sneezed and continued, "No lingering and no one goes to the lavatory till you're all done!" She choked and coughed out hard. Whether it was a blob of saliva or snot she expelled, it flew into the air and landed on the leg of a working table, just where rodents were being gutted. She watched it as it slowly dripped down to the floor.

Out of frustration, without warning as per her character, Food-Killer picked up two squashy tomatoes and threw them towards one weary-looking cook. The tomatoes were plumped to the size of small pumpkins. She missed her target, and the tomatoes hit the wall, splattering. Only a few seeds spurted onto the back of the young ogress's head. The monster-cook was alarmed, but she knew exactly what she had to do: speed up!

Food-Killer had not given up yet. She hastily dug her hand into the tomato basket, ransacking it for the most desirable selections to flick a second shot. The other hand was busy flapping away fruit flies that were agitating to assemble onto the sticky juice of sploshed tomatoes. At the same time, she tried to keep her posture in balance so as not to drop her cloak. Its fastener was too loose and kept detaching. It had been faulty for time out of mind, but she never made any great deal out of it, not for an instant. She used the cloak as was, on all occasions, and it had been years.

"*Ha...a... ash...tish...o-o-o-o!*" She sneezed all of a sudden, drawing back her hand abruptly from the tomatoes. She had to quickly catch her sliding cloak. "You're very lucky!" she called out to the junior cook. "Watch out though! Catch you vegetating again..." she warned, and at least wiped off the mucus mess left on her face with the hem of her cloak.

She started humming an unknown song, obviously only popular to her, and perhaps few other cooks who could decode the dull notes. Her mind seemed to be at peace while purring the tune, but her eyes never stopped wandering.

"I need water... somebody!" Food-Killer called out after a lapse of few minutes. The mood for music had sloughed off. In a trice, two monster-cooks channelled to her at the same time from different ends. Both their ostrich eggshells were full to the brim.

She looked up in surprise. "Am I being ambushed?"

She pulled her legs down, off the cask. "One monster at a time, please! ... Don't want the water anymore, will go get it myself at the rightful time," Food-Killer declared with a condescending look on her face – striking her foot on the floor.

Other cooks in the pool sniggered; they failed abysmally to hold back the urge. They were lucky enough to get away with it scot-free, or perhaps Food-Killer just did not fully register the goings-on.

She went on to fetch the water and flumped back onto her seat.

"If the gods forsake me, honestly, I'll die of headache fissures before the end of the day," she mumbled, drinking her water slowly.

Two loads more of pumpkin heads were carted into the kitchen by a giant leader of the assistance squad. Food-Killer rose up again, going over to suss out the delivery.

"Okay... we have full moon giant pumpkins here. What's in the other sack?" she asked the giant, whilst already tearing the sack open.

"It's the warty goblin," the hulky male mammoth responded *tout de suite*. Food-Killer scowled, tightening her lips – probably suppressing nasty words that were trying to spurt convulsively out of her mouth. She must have been anticipating something else... or perhaps a much larger quantity. Her bodily actions did not reveal much. Using sign language, she implored the crew doing pumpkins to come and get their bulk. Her seat seemed to be screaming her name – calling for her return. She gravitated towards the call.

The monster head cook kept lashing out as she roamed her sharp, scary eyes around while roosting her feet. She wore an intolerant face most of the time and whenever she shouted the cooks panicked. They really never got used to her scolding behaviour, so spillages and breakages also escalated.

The rebellious ones would become frenzied, secretly engaging in food fights as a subtle sign of protest and to entertain themselves throughout, but it never slowed them down. They made shapes of funny objects out of tubers or anything else that drew their eye; chipping them indirectly and impressing odd nicks, which spurred some humour.

Notwithstanding, it was a 'must never get caught' kind of game. Food fights would cost someone a heavy price! It would result in one having to dodge cooking sticks or pans thrown at them, or – the worst – being denied lunch! Nobody would ever wanted to miss lunch on Boisterous Day, especially after toiling for it to be finally sitting on a plate. Whatever happened in the kitchen was not supposed to distract the cooks from working fast. Dawdling was totally unacceptable on such a special day!

# 6

**M**oths flew around peacefully in the Behemoth food storeroom. Removing or shifting any food packages prompted them to go even more maniacal. Back in the kitchen, ears were fed with staccato audio – *'Buzz...zz...zz'* everywhere, over and over. Flies of different kinds were having a party. It was Boisterous Day for them too!

Gadflies and houseflies were mostly concentrated on raw food that was being prepared, especially around the meat carving area. Stray flies were insanely scrounging around walls and doors, and window panes, where they were clustered like abstract pieces of art. Green bottles and blue bottles were drawn to the drum with intestines. 'Zz...*plop*...zz...*plop-plop'* the unlucky ones fell into the huge drum and other cauldrons that were boiling on the crackling fire outside. Nobody ever cared about pests on this side of the world; they literally co-existed. In the main hall they also shared space with bats. A colony of them stayed cosied up in roof corners of the room, divided into smaller groups. The creatures only showed off their full presence at night.

Suddenly!

The deep noise of droning bees went ablaze.

*Oh goodness...* It was mare flies! They were swooping for dear life. The monster head cook stomped towards the preparation area outside, next to the cooking pots where the flies were having their own banquet. The poor insects would not have known that their lives were completely out of danger – Food-Killer was up to intensifying food flavours, nothing more. She had a variety of packs containing spices and herbs, randomly packed in a wooden box. It showed that she knew each and every packet by her fingertips; she never took any time to check out anything. She devilled the powders – handfuls – into all the cooking pots, and went drum to drum too, repeating the same procedure.

She yelled out for wild leeks and a male cook showed up in no seconds, holding a large bowl, heaped up. For the first time since early morning, Food-Killer smiled in appreciation. It revealed how elegantly expansile her mouth could be, which accentuated a hint of charm that was on her face. "How many are they," she asked in a fruity tone, and the figure that was dropped made her even happier. Eighteen. She threw the whole load of segmented leek bulbs into the meat drum.

Before sitting down, she went to the storeroom to probe how many carcasses were still to be skinned and chopped up. She was even further elated at the job that was moving smoothly. There was only a small number left. "If it wasn't for me in the forefront... arm-twisting them," she swore, bunching up a fist with a creased forehead. She snickered afterwards, all alone that time in the storeroom.

On walking out, she glimpsed a bag that looked abandoned. It was sitting on the bottom shelf, on the other side of the room. It just stood out. There was hardly anything meaningful in that area. The package was densely caked with greasy dust. It had not been touched in a very long time; it was a no-brainer. She tried sweeping off the dirt with her fingers and nothing fell off. The bag was sealed, and was much larger than all the other spice packs. She grabbed it with both hands. It was difficult to tell what it was, owing to the sticky grime, but the contents were powdery... kind of brownish in colour.

She went on to open it. The middle part was red and only the outer sections were brown. The bag had surely sat there for an extended period of time. Food-Killer was not a bit concerned. She scrunched up the open top and gave the bag a thorough shake, exerting all her monstrous muscular strength.

She opened it again and closely examined the powder – then shovelled in her finger, taking some and licked at it. The food master right away reached for a larger spoon. She scooped a good deal of it up and gave it a good swirl in her mouth.

"Our meals are done! Done-done-*haute cuisine*! Perfect Boisterous dishes." She was in sheer happiness. She had not even finished swallowing all of it and it puffed out of her mouth as she spoke. "Ghost pepper chillies... can't believe it!" she called out to her juniors, most of who just managed contorted frozen smiles. "What?" She gaped at them. "You don't know much about chillies, right... beyond your ken? You have a lot to learn I see and, of course, I'll TEACH YOU!" Food-Killer took the bag with the precious powder and went back, all-fired up, to the cooking pots. "This is the only thing that was missing," she announced. "Ghost pepper chilli powder; it costs an arm and a leg." Oh, she gave a generous chuck, forming a gunky blanket on the surface of the pots.

"What?" she snarled. Her eyes had turned red, as had her tongue, a shade close to that of her precious powder. She narrowed her brows before continuing with her talking. "The chilli been sitting for a while – it might have lost a little heat. Better SAFE than sorry!" she told the monster-cooks who were showing question marks on their faces. They were left even more appalled.

The only face that was not present amongst the kitchen crew was that of Monster-Starwartle. She was yet to arrive. Starwartle was the youngest of all the monsters, but a well-respected part of the kitchen staff regardless. The young monster had been sent far-off to Acardia Mountains to go and pick mushrooms. She had been tasked the day before, and had not stepped her foot at Behemoth for the Boisterous fiesta as yet. She'd left for Acardia very, very early in the morning, straight from crawling out of bed. There was a list she had been given with the specific types of mushrooms she ought to find. Monster-Starwartle also knew it was a must, filling the enormous baskets, or else trouble! There were two. Thank goodness, she had four arms and four bulgy eyes; double gifted. One set of eyes sat in the centre of her face, and the other centre back of her head. Her stipulated task seemed viable.

# 7

Those who were doing food preparations were after completing their tasks as early as they could. They were twitchy to join the others in the hall and surely they were missing out already.

In an hours' time, Behemoth Hall was thronged with monsters of different shapes and characters. There was one distinctive common feature amongst them – 'bloodcurdling'. They were all hulking and ferocious looking, including the younger ones. Some monsters were grossly overweight but, surprisingly, they seemed to be full of energy as they easily manoeuvred around. It was by no accident either that the Behemoth building had an abnormally high roof. The majority of the monsters present at the festival were both corpulent and extraordinarily tall – towering almost to the height of reaching the roof trusses.

The monsters wore spectacular costumes that dangled with blinding bespoke spangles. It was more like a dress up competition – a fight for the belle of the ball title. The attires were of different cuts and styles. Some were outsize whilst others appeared emphatically tight – their bodies were squeezed in in such a way that exposed all their secret folds, including the lumps and bumps of excess flesh. Regardless of some being distinctly uncomfortable in their inapposite clothing, the celebrations had to go on. Only a handful of them managed to strike a balance. Ghoulishly styled pieces of clothing were sticking out too on quite a number of individuals. As creepy and spine-tingling as it was, this was a monsters' festival! They swanked within the large cluster.

An ogress who was standing next to Monster Avid-Thwack stuck out the most. She was choking in a high necked dress made of dense cotton fabric. It was ash-grey in colour – tight from the neck area going down to the waist. On the back of the dress was a long-frilled train, which also had colossal green ribbons that drooped like lethargic snakes. A series of animal skull studs were riveted onto the frill, and they ran up all the way to the waistline. The bodice of the dress had funnel-shaped sleeves that flared from the elbow, moving down to wrist.

What made it more intriguing was the ogress's finger nails. Apart from being very long, they were corneous and dark purple. The nails protruded from the hem of the funnel sleeves, and she kept flaunting them as she spoke. They indicated a super ability to effortlessly tearing down any ravening predators. The giantess looked rather narcissistic. It was, however, mitigated by her graceful sauntering, unspoiled by having to hoist the heavy dress around everywhere she graced with her presence.

King Jack-eyed wore his large crescent-shaped glasses. The Colossus manta was mandatory. It was meant to be worn by the kings and all respected ogres, especially at important functions like Boisterous celebrations. He wrapped it around his shoulders and secured it with a metallic woggle, which had a condor symbol engraved on it. The manta drooped down his body, covering his entire upper back and part of his upper arms. This superior manta was made of dense alligator skin – very long and partially raw. It was in its original colour of grey-white. The bony-armours and the tail part had never been removed, making the manta silently command respect, as if it still lived on the body of the animal. The rarity of the manta made it extremely striking.

Astonishingly, Fiery-Fireball was simply wearing a vest, with nothing else on the top. It was of loose-fitting cotton material, and deep red in colour. Around his waist was a hide pouch securely tied with plant fibre strings. In the pouch he kept numerous small pellets and a launching pipe, for his odd tasks.

Monster-Monsleek was in her crown – beaming like a legitimate goddess of the primeval forest. She had got the crown at the previous year's festival for being the most popular ogress, voted for by all attendees who were present on the day. It had blunt thorn spikes on the upper top and cured petals all around it. It suited her sometimes charismatic demeanour. Other than that, it fed her desire to look sophisticated, standing out above all the other giantesses. As for her general attire, she was sensationally dressed in a short beige skirt of lace material with a shiny textile underneath. The skirt had exaggerated ankle-length silk fringes attached on the top; beige in colour too. Blobs of beads were fastened on the end of every fringe. They were brown and light in weight. A matching sleeveless beige top completed her stupendous look.

Every ogress was in jewellery. They did not disappoint in displaying assorted kinds, bringing out the rarity in each of them. They made their own, making use of precious gems and colourful stones. Necklaces of seashells and animal teeth were also very popular. This exceptional day was an opportunity for them to show off the exquisite pieces they had created in the year. In addition to neck pieces, they wore the precious valuables around their heads, waists, wrists and on ankles. On those with four arms or more, it was overwhelming. The mingling of dangling jewellery created various tunes as they went up and about tittle-tattling, ahead of the main celebrations.

Monster Avid-Thwack wore a conspicuous brooch, made from vampire fish teeth – the Payara fangs! The kings looked sophisticated, adorned with gargantuan neck pieces with carvings of their status symbol, the condor vulture.

Another note of distinction was the fusion of several strong fragrances, which was very intense. It stretched over to the streets, and the smell would surely make an indelible memory on an average being, should they have walked past on the road during the time.

# 8

A formal welcoming statement was then extended by King Jack-eyed as he officially opened the ceremony. He looked fatigued and his eye-blink was somewhat dull, quite the opposite to his appearance in the earlier hours during arrivals.

All the same, Monster Freaky-Buddy, as the very special guest, was requested to perform what he had lined up for them as the special opening act for Boisterous.

The gruesome four-armed monster hailed from Teras kingdom. He was the reigning king of the faraway and secluded monster-kingdom. He was the one who'd come leading the few invited Teras ogres for the Colossus Boisterous celebrations. In scale and population, Colossus was approximately four times larger than Teras.

The Teras ogre trudged to the front, making brattling sounds with every footstep. Wooden clogs were affixed to the soles of his shoes. He officially greeted the congregants before going up onto the stage to throw his performances. He gave a sincere bow after a short and sweet speech, followed by a roaring shout of their mantra... "Like our condor..." and everyone sang along with him finishing it off, "... fearless we unfurl and soar!"

Thereupon, up he went! The audience could not have waited for any longer. Freaky invited his Teras team to join him for the first two acts.

Monster-Jumbo was also there, in his T-shirt, disoriented still. It was tightly wrapping his neck, but he never appeared to be uncomfortable. The entire squad was very entertaining. They performed with all their souls, and the crowd went blood-and-guts, exhorting 'huzzah-huzzah'. Most of them were up on their feet. The creaking wooden floor did not disturb the flow of deliverance. After the second rendition of their comic play, the group immediately stepped down, tromping back to their seats, leaving Freaky-Buddy alone. The audience was left in hysterics... the comic performance had been out of this world. A terrific act for Boisterous Day!

Freaky had to do his solo act of tap-dancing. He didn't dillydally and straight away broke into their anthem – **Monster Fear!** He sang his heart out whilst tap-dancing. He swayed all his arms around, vacillating them in different directions, and his feet were clacking at a fast pace, showcasing their own polished style. It proved he had thoroughly practised, anticipating only to please. The crowd was kept aflutter and they joined in, singing along.

*Monster fear, Monster fear....*
*We rule the world with Monster fear....*
*We conquer the world with Monster terror....*
*Monster fear, Monster fear....*
*Who is the hector of predators?*
*In my face tell me now....*
*Victorious hector of predators*
*Monster fear, Monster fear....*

'Tatta...ta...ta...tatta...' the front of his shoes went, followed by the heels, 'Clippety-clop...clop...clop', as he clacked on the wooden floor of the platform. 'Tatta...ta...ta...tatta clippety-clop...clop...clop'. He went on with the staccato beat, keeping the crowd mesmerised. After a length of time, he danced to the back end of the platform and, from a huge box, he pulled out a flute. Giving a really good smile at the enchanted monster faces, he embedded the woodwind instrument into his mouth, playing the Monster Fear tune. The sound of the flute brought about such beautiful warmth, which leavened the majestic aura in the room even further.

'Tatta...ta...ta...tatta...'

His body wobbled a bit with staying in control, as the legs fought to keep in motion, to blend with the Monster Fear rhythm. Nevertheless, he did not stop! It was absolutely amusing to his fellow peers, especially how his feet were able to carry the whole massive body he had, keeping it in balance, and how at the same time they kept moving. He danced like he was under gyroscopic effect, that of a spinning top. They were all in awe and very proud.

Monster-Monsleek was drunk at this point in time. She staggered to the front, going towards the platform – *oops* rumbling all the way. She never turned her head. Friends tried to seize her attention but, alas, she was determined to get something resolved. Her foot missed the second step as she tried to climb up to the high place, making the giantess stumble about. She tumbled over onto the floor. She struggled hard to keep herself composed.

"Just come back and sit down. Oh, stop it, Monsleek!" an irritated voice bellowed from one end of the hall, triggering other monsters to also shout. What she was really after, nobody knew. She sat where she had fallen for a while. Fringes of her skirt formed an umbrella, wide and grand around her, making her appear angelic. Nobody would have thought otherwise at that instant. She looked like a botanic pistil of the *Hibiscus Coy-beauty* flower, cocooned in the centre of its broadly bright petals.

Fellow giants swept their eyes back to their special guest who was still performing. They hummed melodiously in buffered voices as he continued blowing the flute. Some danced along lightly and only a few were mere spectators, drinking to the good vibe.

Without warning, Monster-Monsleek finally climbed up onto the stage, taking everybody by surprise. Some had anticipated she wanted to join Freaky-Buddy and probably dance benignly alongside him, although she had not been flashed the green light to by the responsible figures.

Monsleek swayed over to Freaky and tried to grab the very flute he was playing. Freaky-Buddy was struck with shock, like everyone else in the audience... He held tightly to the instrument. "Everybody in the hall is enjoying my rendition!" the Teras ogre bawled in Monsleek's face.

"Hey Freaky-Buddy, let go!" Monsleek screamed and got pushier. "Who do you think you are, Freaky...? It's me and only me... I play the flute!" Monsleek grunted as she poked Freaky-Buddy's arms with her long, crooked nails. Freaky tried holding her back, but she was in no state to back down as yet.

"It's still my time, Colossus queen," he tried reasoning with her, but he was evidently drowning slowly – anger consuming the better of him. The female giant flaunted her pretty whiskered snout around like it had been the culprit, twitching to play the instrument.

"You don't belong here, Freaky.... you're horrid" she pestered on and on, in a stuttering voice. Her sensory hairs were all up erect.

The merciless Freaky-Buddy got really agitated. His underlying colours were now surfacing, unrestrained. He tried scratching Monsleek in the face with his claws but kept missing.

"Argh... you think I'm scared of you, Teras monster?" Monsleek guffawed!

They went on scuffling for few more minutes and finally the flute dropped onto the floor and Monsleek picked it up quickly.

"Got you!" the ogress exclaimed, giving the Teras monster a smack on the head with it before shoving it inside her blouse.

"Tell you what, I was so smitten by you, but I realise my brain's only been fooling me. I've had serious thoughts of marrying you, Monster-Monsleek, but you're no good at all." With those last words, Freaky dug his corneous nails into Monsleek's fur. "You're the worst!" he added.

"Go on lord king – go on and let's see where your energy reserves can take you," Monster-Monsleek giggled. "Teras folks are weak." Her voice had surprisingly gained momentum.

"Oh whacky!" Freaky-Buddy was further provoked. All his four arms got busy. "You'll be sorry for your words." He pinched, slapped and tried to reach for Monsleek's nose, but could not access it. She kept dodging.

"Oh, don't stop... go deeper and pull out all the ticks buried in my skin!" Monster-Monsleek went delirious, spewing irksome words as she fought back and tried to hide her face, all at the same time.

"Silly Monsleek, come down now! Get off the plat–"

"Oh, no, please leave Monsleek alone. Did you hear what Freaky-Buddy just said to her?" one monster called out, with another quickly interjecting, and Johnny-Warlock also chimed in here and there. He went up on his feet *preaching*. An ogre who was sitting down below him just did not realise that Warlock was speaking, waving a stick that was in his hands dangerously, and it seemed it would hit the poor ogre on the middle of his head.

"Of course, not to happen, perhaps in the next era! He can't marry Ogress Monsleek. Just imagine having Freaky as your husband. Is that not a boring imagery to one's mind?" Although lame, Warlock aired his own thoughts, making sure his point was crystal clear.

"What!? No... no... don't even go there, I beg. It's torture for the mind to synthesise any of that," a Colossus giantess blazoned out.

Fiery-Fireball escalated the squabble, echoing the same sentiment. "Of course not, certainly. Monster-Monsleek belongs here, and nobody comes to take her away, and surely not Freaky-Buddy!"

"Yeah, maybe when pigs fly..." said Warlock, agreeing.

"Our Queen Monsleek-Monster goes nowhere we don't approve of..." cried Avid-Thwack. "Are there no ogresses there in Teras? Tell me," she lamented looking at Fiery-Fireball.

"Valid verdict, Avid-Thwack. Valid, hats off!" Fiery responded, firing up tensions that were stewing.

"Ridiculous! Don't be stuck in conformity. You ought to loosen up folks," a Teras guest announced. "What's wrong with Freaky-Buddy? He's a king after all – and look at me; how many – spit it out – how many of you here in Colossus have beautiful bodies like mine?" she trumpeted unhesitatingly and stood up, showing off her body structure.

"What's really your intention with the shimmy walk?" a middle-aged Colossus lass scolded. Her face clearly reported she was really stung.

"Not so silly for you to ask," the Teras ogress turned up the whites of her eyes answering back. "Must I goose-step then?" she continued with her flippant statements and went on ramming her feet onto the floor – marching back and forth like a bouncer, provokingly. It made the Colossus Monster-Damsel fly off the handle.

"I mean, we have more than enough buxom figures here. Excuse me, you can sit down! I'm sassy too; you didn't take a good look at me right... or maybe I am too blinding to your eyes? We also have large earlobes and I have triangular shaped ones. After all, we have more than two arms, the majority of us here in Colossus!"

The goose-stepping Teras ogress had seemingly plugged her ears. She transformed from marching to sashaying – and she went all the way to the main door and back, with her hands clutched to her waist. Her necklace jounced hip to hip, going the opposite way to her swinging motion. The necklace was very long and weighty. It had a beautiful glitter-red animal bone wedged in the centre.

"You're really up to something, aren't you?" the Colossus lass called out to her in a goring voice, distracting the hurly burly that was hatching in the hall for a few seconds.

"Look at our Monster-Monsleek; she's just like those beauties we hear about – a living translation of enchantresses in fairy tales!" She spoke her mind, and matters went into complete disarray thereafter!

The master of ceremonies was nowhere to be seen!

On the stage, the fight was ongoing and getting vicious. The two were positioned at a halfway point from the coffered piece of artwork, and the mounted lion was glaring down at them menacingly, as if life were now breathing in it. Nobody in the crowd went up to stop the fight, since random visits to the platform where strictly prohibited. They held on to the rule, awaiting a move or instruction from the senior members who had dashed out for a quick meeting at their usual rendezvous.

Monster Freaky-Buddy's claws went even deeper!

"Argh, that's very tingly, Freaky..." Monster-Monsleek went on gushing her sarcastic remarks. In an instant she turned slightly and flared up an astonishing somersault at warp speed. Right away she snapped out of Freaky's grip and ran into the crowd. Freaky-Buddy went after her and also disappeared in the multitude.

Fellow monsters, however, continued with their own squabbling. Some thought Monster-Monsleek needed to be disciplined and others disputed that she was one of them and said it would be uncivil to drag her name through the mud. They all shouted and chanted at the same time. Everything was out of control.

"Hey! Hey! We came here to enjoy the festival... Boisterous Festival after all. What's this havoc for now?" the Teras monsters complained in unison.

"Monsleek, what were you trying to do precisely? You're wrong – you're wrong and it's a no-brainer. You instigated all of this!" Johnny-Warlock was on his feet bewailing, and a good number of Colossus monsters backed him. It was perplexing, though, how he had all of a sudden changed his mind from being a supporter of Monster-Monsleek to now condemning her behaviour. Quarrels over other trivialities escalated, however, and all culminated in physical fights. There was commotion in Behemoth Hall thereafter, which was worsened by clamouring sounds of objects. Shrill cries had become the predominant language uttered in the cluster. In other smaller sections there were shatters of crazy giggles. In no time, blood had squirted onto the walls. A few candles were left snuffed out too, and the dripping wax was now camouflaged by blood. They spat and bellowed, and the hurly-burly ruptured to the streets.

*'Boom! Boom! Boom!'*
Music started blasting.
*'Bam!!'*
The sound became deafening as the volume rose to a crescendo.

Monster Treble-Blare had just brought in a stereo on the assumption that music would calm the situation. The sound went even higher and higher, yes, but the giants turned more boorish and unruly. They found the alien notes very disruptive to their ongoing debates. They raised their voices to try and surpass the gizmo, but alas, its volume knob was finally glued to the maximum. They wondered who had irrationally granted him the power to clamber onto the stage with such an ugly object. In as much as it fell dismally short to do anything of substance, Treble-Blare's body and brains responded resoundingly well to the raucous tune. His back was arched, and his head drawn closer to the stereo – his eyes were completely shut. Fellow giants tried waving. They climbed up on the rustic chairs and benches, hollering that he should discard his *whatever* gizmo, but he was lost in his own world. Anything else just did not matter anymore. The relinquishing of the stereo remained a war on its own – isolated from a string of other wars that had already imbued Behemoth!

'*What*...?'
'*Where*...?'
'*Who*...?'
'*Why*....?'
King Jack-eyed was puzzled...

He did not know *what* to do or *where* to start off from. Neither did he know *who* to ask nor how at least to be in a position to establish *why* such disorder had broken out on such a very special day. The root of the problem was that he himself had become drunk. He was entirely blitzed. There was no way he could have fulfilled the hefty duties of Behemoth master of ceremonies.

The ogre commander had embarked on his drinking session in the wee hours of the festival. He had turned mellow and virtually become part of the audience. He only ended up shouting, "Hey!" and his head looked too heavy for his body. He struggled to hold it in place, but his glasses were still on his face, just hanging loose. The monster-king could not lift up any of his six arms and he ended up waving only his fingers. *East – west, east – west, east...* gently, he kept going mawkishly.

# 9

**M**onster Food-Killer presupposed food would bring some peace. Back in the kitchen, work was moving pretty well. Most of the primary dishes were done and ready.

She dashed to the kitchen and took a huge casserole dish. It was full of steaming snails and lizards, immersed in gelatinous creamy-yellow soup. She placed the dish in the centre of the hall and thrust her hands into a pile of serving equipment. It was stashed just above her head in the trusses. Eagerly, she pulled out the largest ladle. She wiped off the dust with her apron. The ladle had the longest handle, which had a decorative symbol of the condor vulture on the tip. It had its graceful wings wide open. All the dishing equipment had the same design. Some were hung by the wing design part.

With the prime ladle in her hands, *goody-goody!* she was ready to serve. Food-Killer really wanted to impress, and all the attention became hers. Her prediction had been spot-on.

"Boisterous hors d'oeuvre," she happily announced as she opened the lid.

"Keep your buccal cavities open folks... catch the scrummy starter!" the food boss instructed in a hoarse voice. Her words were well received with great appreciation. Enthusiastically, she started scooping up the food – a heap at a time – and randomly threw it over to the congregants. Many of the individuals who had gone off the premises hurried back at the call of food aromas that were wafting enticingly in the air.

Having waited impatiently for hours, they now ate hungrily. As for the irksome fights, it seemed that food had been a miraculous quencher.

"*Schwamalalakakka!*" Monster-Jumbo cried out with sensational enjoyment. "This is a perfect ten," he praised in a husky voice. "The heat... hey! My palate has been rejuvenated." The Teras giant sang on, waiting for another turn.

"Welcome to Colossus!" Monster-Monsleek interposed, winking at him.

A few others expressed their emotions too, and conversations had begun shifting slowly. They now revolved around food.

"Out of ten, I score her fifteen," another voice belted in the room. Food-Killer went all exuberant doing her job.

"Come back this side!" monsters all yelled at the same time, in different sitting areas, and their food master did not disappoint.

"Yes, yes... wide – just keep 'em open!"

Her ladling tempo intensified. Every ounce of her body was busy rendering support simultaneously to the ladling hands. All her muscles vibrated nonstop.... A string of her apron unexpectedly dived into the casserole, and she noticed it right away. She drew it out irritably, and some soup speckled onto her upper arm. She mopped it off with her tongue and continued working!

"I rather prefer frogs that are cooked on direct fire."

"You mean *Frog Picante Barbeque,* right?"

Monster Fiery-Fireball aired his own views and Monster-Oblivious, from the Teras kingdom, responded, smirking.

"I love those too," she went on – and raised her hand as if to affirm with an oath. "Our food master in Teras does those for us, all the time, every celebration. Oh, you must taste them," she convinced.

"Nah, I got you covered, Fiery-Fireball," Food-Killer, the juggler barged in. "They've already put up a fire for that. It's sparking blue and red right now. Consider it done!" She gave a rictus grin to Monster-Oblivious. "I allocated two dishes-full just for that." She elevated her hand, stretching out two fingers, and again mentioned, "Two," *sotto voce* – widening her eyes.

Sweat had begun seeping out gradually on Food-Killer's forehead. She was extremely busy.

Fine and dandy, it all played out in the first substantial minutes until Johnny-Warlock, who was belching and calmly cleaning his ears, started buffeting a table out of anger. It was worth being grateful that the wooden table survived, not splitting apart and giving in to his rage. He was sitting right in the corner of the hall amongst a few other ogres.

"My face, Food-Killer, come on... I said look at my face!" With his fists he went on bashing the guiltless piece of wood.

All of a sudden, warts on his face had been exposed. A ladleful of soup had accidentally splashed onto his forehead, washing off his make-up.

"How do I even remove your greasy soup off my face now?" His heart was thumping fit to shatter. The mess was just too embarrassing for his ego. Boisterous Day was yet to be over and surely there had to be a 'great looking' annotation against his name in all Boisterous celebration records.

"This was deliberate, right?" he asked, glaring at the dripping soup, popeyed. Its colour made him jitter with fury. The creamy-yellow soup was clearly mixed with bits of his clay make-up. It had happened, he knew it – yes: warts now exhibited and becoming a hotspot. They were many and blatantly popping out. A crust of special clay always redeemed his ego and no other monster knew what lay beneath and beyond his face coverings.

"I had not even called for some more!" he complained notches higher, fuelling up his anger to an upper zone. His teeth were chattering, and blood vessels on the sides of his neck were throbbing.

In his visibly shaking hand, he tightly squeezed a baton-stick, as if to break it. It was the one he had been using to dewax his ears. He appeared completely incognisant of how disgustingly sludgy it was. Given the phenomenally large ears he had, Johnny-Warlock made cleaning sticks for his ears out of tree branches. He would then tie a cloth on one end to create a just-comfortable blob. In any small, quiet chance he got to himself, cleaning his ears became his amusement. Everywhere he went, he took a stick or two with him.

Food-Killer continued serving starving tummies, snubbing the maddened fellow. Johnny-Warlock could not hold his anger any longer. He snuffled deeply and stood up clumsily, like he had had too much to eat. Everything was in Food-Killer's recording. She closely followed every move from the corner of her eye as she carried on with her devoted service.

The bossy giantess finally smelt a rat. She was now shuddering. Anxiety seemed to have spun through her. Although she tried hard not to show it, it was just too visible to be concealed. Monster Food-Killer never wanted her own self-image bruised either.

With no warning, Johnny-Warlock threw his baton stick in question towards her.

She ducked!

Aimed at her face, the stick mistakenly dropped into the casserole dish.

"Oops... that was close. *Whew...* "Food-Killer sighed with an annoying titter.

Johnny-Warlock left his sitting place right away and stamped going over to where she was serving from.

Food-Killer, on the other hand, did the unimaginable. She promptly heaved the large casserole dish and scarpered outside.

Right to the close-by street, the giantess proceeded in no time. She crouched behind a large cactus bush, not too far from their gate, trying to read what was happening back at Behemoth. There was just a loud, confusing noise... a cacophony of voices, mixed with sounds of rattling equipment and foot stomps, but with no one outside thus far. Within a few seconds she left. She never took any chances.

The Behemoth food master ran down the road. She kept checking her back constantly. *"I'll wash his whole body with this remaining soup if he continues with his nonsense,"* she spoke and laughed loudly at her brilliant idea.

Monster Johnny-Warlock appeared a minute later at the gate. He went after Food-Killer's heels.

A multitude of monsters raced behind them, clamouring! They were after the casserole dish. They thought Food-Killer was being greedy, running away with food.

"We've had enough! Such unruly behaviour earlier on... and now it's the hoggish, horrid Food-Killer!" the monsters remarked whilst running along. Some had picked up pieces of equipment on their way outside. Others threw stones and dry dung after her, but the stout monster simply increased velocity. She streaked even faster. Being already far ahead gave her a great advantage. The goulash was still tucked in her arms. The cloak played a resistance game – flying high up into the air, creating a canopy behind her like it would scoop her off the ground at any second, but forward she kept moving. Her shoes slipped off, but she never stopped.

"Yak!" Food-Killer shouted, but down Monstrosity Street she pounded on and on. "Yak!" Again, she sighed. Her cloak dropped off, but her pudgy hands kept holding tightly to the dish. Oh, she ran meteorically. The knot on her apron strings was slowly dissolving. It grazed constantly against her back with every movement of her body.

Further down, at the end of Monstrosity Street, she reached and turned into Lane Mammuthus. It was a wider and smoother road with no gullies or stones, unlike before. Her eyes were fixed on the road for quite some time. The strings of her apron finally fell apart, and were now wavering in whichever direction was commanded by the air currents.

Later on, upon turning her head – "Oh, trouble!" – Monster Food-Killer realised the huge group was striding after her still. The road had been smoother for them too. They were oncoming like the devil's dust. She wished she had at least three arms, to get a steadier grip of the casserole dish. Her thick and short tail was of no help at this point either.

*"If it were maybe much longer,"* she desired. *"I'd have stretched it – tackled and tripped all of them, one by one... one by one, until they all surrendered and hailed my name."* The voice, although muffled and hiccuppy, was able to articulate what her mind fantasised while her dumpy feet kept thudding on the road. Birds chirped relentlessly up in the trees, probably transmitting a scolding message for the pell-mell to stop. It was a pity though – all the ogre parties were indisputably determined, and it was plausible that the chase would go on

and on endlessly. The mad rush would only have responded to a more aggressive tranquillizer.

"I-I lacerate you with... with my teeth, Food-Ki–" Monster Avid-Thwack panted. She appeared absolutely fatigued and out of breath. "*Whew...*" Avid-Thwack sighed as the skillet she was holding fell onto the ground. She entirely lost her equilibrium and plumped down on her knees, right next to her skillet, gasping for breaths. She fainted. Her companions ran up, panicky, and attended to her. After a few chest compressions she was up! blinking rapidly.

"How could you let Ghost-Hound sit on my chest?" Avid-Thwack was astounded upon waking up to Ghost-Hound's paws resting around her neck. The way he was staring was equivocal; it looked as though his eyes were about to spew venom into Thwack's.

"I could have died, folks," Avid-Thwack twittered. "Ghost-Hound's full senses only feature at night... remember..." Avid was now palpitating.

She was received with peals of giggles. Little had she known that Monster Ghost-Hound had also tumbled into a *worrywart* state, like everyone else there, over her condition.

"That thread of facts stringing from your mouth shows us you're back, you've survived, Thwack." Monster-Monsleek smoothed out all the ruckles of fear that were grossly prominent on Avid-Thwack's face. She plucked a bead on her skirt in-between her fingers and twiddled with it, looking compassionately at Avid-Thwack, who was still flipping her brows endlessly.

"Like our condor – fearless we unfurl and soar!" Another female monster delivered their mantra loudly, with a speck of vanity. A good number of monsters gave up at this point and decided to walk back to the hall, together with Avid-Thwack.

"Give her some meat when you arrive. She loves meat, and maybe water. She may gulp down some water first... *I think*... Really, I don't know, but meat is her favourite. It'll save her, that I know." Monster Fiery-Fireball went on faltering. He was looking at Avid-Thwack too, with sympathetic eyes. She was in the process of rising up and shaking off dust.

Fiery turned his upper body, lunging at the height of one young monster who was behind him, and spoke to her in a muffled voice. "She's just famished, that I'm pretty sure. Check behind the larger boulder at the gate; the one closest to the cactus plant... there's a red brick on the bottom – yeah, behind that brick I put a plastic bag with roasted roaches. Give that to Monster Avid, please..." The young monster nodded to the request.

Avid-Thwack was looking ready to go. "I'll carry my skillet," she said, looking at the ogres encircled around her. Her speech was brittle, but she looked strong enough and eager.

Fiery-Fireball did not stay there for any longer. He and a few others went ahead with the chase – at jet speed! They were more compelled now to help recover the stolen food. Avid-Thwack had almost bad them farewell in the name of the casseroled molluscs!

The larger group of monsters had kept moving meanwhile, going after Food-Killer. They were now heading east, towards Great Colossus Boulevard. It was the very way that led into the Arcane kingdom. Fiery-Fireball's group had a broad gap to cover to catch up with them.

"Just put the food down, hey!" some voices in the larger group screamed.

"Oh, hell's bells! What kind of festival are we to have with only a few bites to share?" a corpulent giantess in an orange canvas dress that had split open on the sides out of pressure, highlighted. She was about threefold the size of a human.

"Not snails' goulash after all," another ogress backed up.

"I heard it's the only lot they prepared!" the corpulent giantess mentioned, stressing out all the urgency.

It boosted their energy levels, and they all increased pace. They went on faster for a good length of time and covered a great distance to catch their food boss.

In not much time, the group had arrived in Arcane kingdom – right in its capital city.

Monster Food-Killer was not to be easily underrated. Affrays later blew up amongst her fellow folks. They had persistently continued hitting each other unintentionally as they tried aiming at her with their various weapons. Coming in full force from right behind was Fiery-Fireball. His smaller group had progressed significantly.

He was the culprit who apparently worsened the situation... taking himself as if he were in a contest of some sort.

The mammoth fished out a handful of pellets. "Gotcha!" he boastfully threatened as he launched them one after the other into the air with the special pipe. However, with obstruction he miscalculated the destination, and the little balls catapulted in wildly different directions, a situation that was worsened by the wind. They sparked off innocent monsters' bodies. The victims yelped and scratched. They tried to keep hitting the road, but suddenly came to a halt. They turned against one another.

# IO

Meanwhile, the monster-king, Jack-eyed, was fighting hard to try and put himself back together at Behemoth. Surrounding him were empty calabashes. He tried kicking the one that seemed closest to him, but his foot failed to rise. It was his hand that slightly ascended instead. As much as he might have wanted to, coming back to the beautiful present remained a challenge. He was still detached. His manta was lying abandoned on the floor, slightly behind the door. He was absolutely ashamed of himself when he caught a glimpse of it.

The very feared twelve-eyed monster, Twelve-eyed, eventually took over as the master of ceremonies. It had been consensually agreed upon, and Jack-eyed was ushered to a secluded place for recovery.

In addition to his tremendous heavy weight, the other alarming attribute of Twelve-eyed lay in his eerie horns. They were very unusual; long in length but yet spiral and marginally slanted towards the front. At the most extreme end, the horns were sharply jagged. *Yikes* – he would easily fit in and mistakenly be counted in the *animalia* kingdom.

Monster Twelve-eyed was such a hell-raiser. If he got really upset or infuriated, with his peculiar spikes he could literally do anything! Troublemakers knew him for giving ruinous penalties.

In no time, Twelve-eyed took out a flail and stood right by the gate. Its shaft was very long and thick. It was made out of wood, finely polished. The flail was his signature weapon. It had a spiked spherical head on its end. It was made of wooden material too, but much heavier, and there was a welded steel-link chain attachment.

He threshed his flail about, looking at it with admiration and flexing his muscles. He cleared his throat repeatedly in the process, to try and attract the giants' attention, but he realised it was not enough yet to stir much change. Those who were close by simply stared with reluctance. He was getting kind of frustrated... losing patience with every tick-tock – then, suddenly, *'Deaush!'* He rammed a century-year-old tree with his flail violently – giving the weapon a warm-up and at the same time inoculating fear into the rumbustious monster attendees. He grubbed out the spiked head that had remained stuck on the tree. Its handle was left swinging loose. He spit onto the spherical head once and gave it a good polish with a small cloth he drew from his back pocket.

The substitute ruler was ready to restore peace. Breakout of sweat on his creased forehead evinced his utter determination to bring the ongoing havoc to a complete rest.

"Ahoy!" he bellowed. The microphone, a gadget he had been given by Monster Treble-Blare, carried his voice, shipping it to very faraway places, reaching even the farthest avenues of Arcane domiciles. All monsters could hear him, including those who were now breathing Arcane air – in the quest for a casserole dish.

"Everybody back to Behemoth or PAY THE PRICE!" Over the wind, the voice kept piercing as he fulminated. "I'm allowing only three minutes for everybody to get settled!" Twelve-eyed venerated the effectiveness of the borrowed voice-enhancing gadget. He had not seen anything like that ever before. The monster head had initially said NO to it after the music incident, but now he would unhesitatingly stand as an advocate. It amplified his vocalization, one word to another, and thence fortified his dominance. He loved it and couldn't be any prouder!

Without thinking twice, all monsters started streaming back to the hall. Nobody dared to try their luck with him. Avid-Thwack, together with a couple of other monsters, rose up promptly too. The team had been benignly basking in the sun, perched on the nearby boulders at the corner of Ogre Street. For poor Monster-Pinniped, a much older ogre, it had been a golden chance for him to attend to his itchy spots, but he had to obey the command.

It got chaotic once again as all the monsters scrambled at both entrances, forcing their way inside. It did not, however, take much time before they'd all sat down and settled. Only the individuals who had reached Arcane kept coming in randomly, in ones and twos.

It was in that time frame that Monster-Starwartle arrived from the mountains. It had surely taken her almost the better half of the day to complete the mushroom picking task. She walked through the hall entranceway.

Glancing at the baskets, almost overflowing with freshly picked mushrooms, monsters could not help it. They dribbled saliva, drooling at the different kinds of fungi that showed distinct layers pretty well through the basket holes. They were all of special kinds that were principally meant for the gods, they believed. They marvelled at how densely packed the massive baskets were, and the baskets also seemed extremely heavy, with their centre parts steeply elevated to the shape that of an anthill top. They kept staring, and Starwartle gave them the blind eye as she briskly walked past, going straight to the kitchen.

With no time to rest, Monster-Starwartle was ordered to go and fetch the casserole dish from Food-Killer, who was still dragging her feet, walking reluctantly outside. Starwartle scampered out immediately. With only a single word – forthwith; she always actioned orders.

Brandishing his flail recklessly back and forth, up and down, back and forth, the now master of ceremonies Twelve-eyed accidentally rived off a heavy, rusty platform fan that dangled loose from the trusses. Upon striking the floor, it shattered apart with an ear-splitting sound. The hall went dead quiet as the breakage sound reverberated. A thick cloud of dust puffed into the air, causing alarm. It was a relief that no one was hurt, but hairs of the furred monsters visibly bristled and nobody uttered a word.

They gave him prominence. Right away, Monster Twelve-eyed ruptured into blustery laughter. It cut through the dead silence, resonating throughout the large hall. He took it as a moment of manifesting his self-importance. No one would dispute his actions. They all gazed at him with desperate anticipation in their eyes – hungry to continue with their celebrations in peace.

Monster-Starwartle returned to the hall, cradling the huge casserole dish. Straight away, she reported back to Monster Twelve-eyed, showing him what had been recovered. The dish was – surprisingly – still half-full. Nothing had spilt in the helter-skelter hours. Twelve-eyed drew out a snail, just one – but large, the perfect size for a full-blown average-human meal. He placed the snail onto his tongue, which was fully stretched out, already awaiting business.

"The taste hasn't changed, thanks to the gods," he certified through the microphone. "That cursed stick must be removed," he admonished, lapping up some soup that was left smeared on his fingers.

Monster-Starwartle safely wrapped the retro cast-iron vessel in her cautious arms to take it to the kitchen. She had to walk dodging the woody pieces, and the iron bolts and nuts of the shattered fan.

She placed the vessel onto the kitchen table and yanked out Monster Johnny-Warlock's baton stick, *tout de suite*. The cloth was swampy, fully deluged with the goulash soup. It's colour of origin had been completely engulfed.

"Now what..."

"Are you going to return it? He easily goes on the rampage. You know him," Monster-Ember, a fellow male cook, inquired inquisitively, glaring at the saturated stick as if he were conversing with it. It had been placed on the bucolic table. Starwartle picked up the sludgy stick within the blink of an eye and channelled it straight to the garbage bin. She went strutting like a peacock. The bin was outside, just by the kitchen door. "He'll get it from there if he so wishes," she declared, and her counterparts simply watched in awe.

It was rib-tickling to a handful of senior monsters. They found it very peculiar – such an authoritative voice emanating from a youngster. A consentaneous agreement was officially made on the flip of a coin, and they now trusted only her to be in charge of all food proceedings for the remainder of the day.

Monster-Starwartle didn't waste any seconds – she paced up all her actions, and walked up and down endlessly, trying to prove her worth and devotion. She rinsed two cloths at once, wrung them and wiped down the long working table in a twinkle.

Her dorsal eyes were fixed on a junior, who was taking forever skinning her batch of frogs; her counterpart was done with hers quite an estimable moment before. As soon as she noticed the scary orbs peering at her, her speed increased – before any word had been verbalized. It were as if the power of the condor had miraculously administered some life into her.

Right after, with her frontal eyes, Starwartle espied two cooks heaving an enormous beast carcase. They were footslogging from the storeroom going outside. "Eureka!" she bawled.

Full of vim, Starwartle scooched down and dragged out a massive crate that was under the table. It screeched all the way out. Inside, were piles of serving platters, all wooden. She lined them up on the table – all her four arms busy. "Bring the intestines!" she barked to the cooks. "I need the grain too!"

"From gloom to animosity," one cook complained discreetly, and walked off with folded arms to the storeroom for a slight phase of recuperation. "A perfect replica of Food-Killer has descended..." another concurred and joined in the hideout. There were many other cooks to do the ordered duties. Despite the fact that they hated it, they had to deliver.

So, without much ado, the drum with intestines was set in front of Monster-Starwartle.

She drew the large cylinder much closer towards her body – driven by a jot of disdain. "Come on, it's Boisterous Day!" the young leader tried to cheer up her now subordinates, as she dug a dishing spoon into the long, curly pipes. The soup had curdled really thick. On lifting up the spoon, she realised she was simply holding its mere handle. She had broken off the scoop in her haste!

She stooped again, rummaging for yet another beneath the table. On coming up, her frontal eyes were still thrust onto the stash of the serving utensils, likely in calculation of which next one she would go for should the second one break too. Instantaneously, her head bumped on the overlapping lip of the drum. It tipped over, hitting a cask with fruit juice! *Food-Killer's early morning foot stool...* The cask was torn apart by the heavy drum, emitting a blasting noise, which startled the team that was tussling with carcasses outside. They came scudding!

The team was received by juice slopping all over the floor, flowing around the clumps of disgorged intestines. The curve of the broken silver scoop reflected, half buried in one of the clumps. Starwartle was left flummoxed.

"Those are supposed to be served hot, aren't they?" she asked. Her tone was thick and suppressed. She had literally raised the point to herself, unfortunately. No one answered. They just stood there, gawping; nobody willing to come forth with any suggestions – she had to know better, she was at the HELM. A culmination of excitement, anxiety and a pain in the head left her hitting her forehead with all four of her hands. She was thrown into a whirl of thinking and thinking and –. She missed Food-Killer – they all did. It was printed all over their faces.

Food-Killer's state of mind obviously gravitated there too – where the pots were moiling, and where she had left the cooking job distressingly quarter way through to completion. Her vocal cords suffered too.... she only got satisfaction and solace in shouting and screaming.

"Frogs burning outside..." Starwartle fumbled for some words after a long interval of twiddling thumbs. Monster-Ember slunk outside, holding a large barbecue fork by its condor wings.

Just then, Fiery-Fireball had been tasked to go and check if everything was going fine in the kitchen. Johnny-Warlock followed behind him, excited. He had probably envisioned himself getting some tasters. Fireball opened the kitchen door, throwing his right foot inside. He walked back instantly, drawing the door gently. He quickly turned to Johnny who was loudly talking frivolous stuff. "Shush..." he whispered. "They're having a serious meeting with Starwartle. Let's not disturb them."

Fiery had been met by Starwartle's prickly dorsal eyes. Johnny stroked his chin with disappointment. They made a U-turn, wending their way back to the hall.

"Starwartle is extraordinary... *you just didn't see it, Warlock*: every cook is there," he breathed. "They're all swarmed around her. All ears... very attentive!" Fireball marvelled, his eyes all lit up, but Johnny-Warlock was not interested in all of that. He looked gutted...

"As long as the meeting doesn't extend to eternity," he remarked indistinctly.

# II

It did not go down well with Food-Killer, receiving the acrid news that young monster-cook Starwartle had temporarily taken over her reins. Nevertheless, she had to accept and co-operate, till when the dust had perhaps settled. It had appeared too harsh to her, for she was not even allowed to make an appearance at either the cooking or the service areas. Totally grumpy and tired, she just sat in the audience, amongst the other ogresses, after she had arrived back from the streets. Just like everyone else in the hall, she was completely unaware of the current situation in the kitchen. They all sat, waiting to be served.

With eyes on each of side of his head, Monster Twelve-eyed could immediately espy any nonsense in the hall before it flamed up. "Whoever causes trouble one more time today... shall LOSE their toes!" Furious, Twelve-eyed maintained his autocratic tone, and his brows were perpetually knitted.

Food-Killer looked at her bare feet and quickly retrieved her shoes to shield them. She had stuffed the shoes into the cloak's pockets.

There was now absolute peace in the hall. Twelve-eyed's ruling formula seemed to be working seamlessly, and the degree of orderliness promised to remain ceaseless.

After only about fifteen minutes, he reached for the microphone again. He gave it a whang on the head a couple of times... doing a sound test, taking it cubits farther from what he had been instructed. The reflection of the sounds was unendurable. His ear and side eyes were fixed right there by the mouthpiece as he whanged it repeatedly. He was incognisant that he ought to be extra gentle with the gadget; there were already worn-out points along its cord. Thin wires were bulging out through torn parts of the insulation sheath.

Spinning the magical gadget around with only two hands, he took five – six – steps getting closer to the crowd as if he intended to whisper. In that instant, the mic was planted onto his mouth.

"Repeating myself I don't and never will..."

It prompted snickering in the crowd, which went unnoticed by him. He went on talking, with his voice gravelly, like there was a frog clenching in his throat. "Reserve your claws for only their intended purposes; for the gods' sake..." His eyes on the left side spear-pointed directly at the Teras king.

Monster Freaky-Buddy, however, appeared not to have taken much of it in. His attention was invested onto the luscious looking *Frog Picante Barbeque* he had just been given. Steam was still swirling from the dish – served hot, coming straight from the smoky flames! The frogs were pinned in a row, one after the other – six of them – onto long-thin sticks that were harvested from the woods. They were arranged on adorned coconut shells. As the very special guest, Freaky-Buddy had been served first. He had three sticks on his plate – eighteen frogs. It was Boisterous!

Twelve-eyed kept throwing reminders at regular intervals going forward. He managed to preserve his consistence and the absolute grip. "Voting process is now officially open, folks. All I can say is – vote wisely. We have the whole afternoon, so take your time. Only go when you feel you're ready... otherwise immerse yourselves in the delightful lunch that's forthcoming. I don't want any horrid noises end-to-end – no excuses please, lest we upscale to HEFTIER PENALTIES!" the chief monster huffed.

It was a very important announcement that had been conveyed by Twelve-eyed. Colossus habitants could now cast their votes for their favourite candidate to be the king for the oncoming new year. There was a list of potential candidates, seconded publicly beforehand – a process that was open to the entire Colossus monster population. On Boisterous Day, every individual had to simply write down the number of their preferred candidate, according to their official numbers as listed on a board. Twelve-eyed's name also appeared on the pivotal list, placed two names below the reigning king, Jack-eyed.

Post the crucial announcement, Twelve-eyed slowly turned around once – a *365* degree turn – looking down at his feet, respiring heavily. He showed to have been thinking really hard.

"Oh, we're grateful to our cooks for their wondrous work... the food is luscious, I must admit," he noted immediately after taking the breather. The announcement flipped over a tense feeling that was looming in the air in just few pulsations. "There's a lot to feast on..." Twelve-eyed further cited and gave a contagious grin, which left fellow monsters aflutter and licking their lips. "...Don't know why we tend to forget mentioning the most crucial matters," he pointed out, looking kind of disappointed in himself. The hands that were not busy on the microphone were radiating on the belly, rubbing it gently, throughout... as the mouth formulated the delicious words.

Out of the blue, Twelve-eyed fell back into his tyrannical behaviour. He lowered his head to a confrontational clash position, and went on to sway it robustly, for a minute or so, with his horns moving apace in a circular motion. All his twelve orbs bulged out to the size matching that of large marbles. It were as if they would drop out of their sockets at any given second.

HE MEANT BUSINESS. He expected no nonsense to crop up.

"Like our condor – fearless we unfurl and soar!" Twelve-eyed finished off his delivery with their motto, before ensconcing himself back into the leader's comfy seat. It was a huge chair with a sturdy wooden frame, brown in colour and upholstered with thick padding. On its back lay the open wings of the condor vulture, slightly curved inwards like brackets; to offer a serene feel and some protection to the king. All in all, the seat simply portrayed superiority of stature.

Food had been placed in front of Twelve-eyed – plenty of it. Monster-Starwartle and her team had been shrewd; they'd put ample servings of each and every thing they had cooked onto the high table. An embellished ostrich eggshell filled up with juice was also set on the side, just for Twelve-eyed. He vehemently refused the fermented beverage. He had to tread carefully, especially after Jack-eyed's huge blunder.

Lunch was subsequently brought out to everyone else, as they went in slowly to deposit their ballots.

Twelve-eyed stretched out an arm and snaffled the microphone by its tail, pulling it over. It was a distance from him. Not by the smallest chance would he find himself compelled to leave his cosy seat unnecessarily. He clenched the microphone with all his hands, crippling any prospects of it escaping from his greasy hands. "Keep in mind, relations are merely an empty vessel that can only be quelled with food." He blared out the tantalising words of wisdom to the congregants as the food was being served around.

He quickly discarded Treble-Blare's gadget far away from his reach and continued relishing the meal, escaping into his own small world of flavours and textures.

How the kitchen monsters rescued themselves from the quandary remained a mystery. It had been very nasty but the pretty basil flowers popping out on each and every platter spoke a whole different story. The simple garnish hyped up the appearance of the food to a top-notch level, leaving the bumpy phase of preparations a secret between the cooking crew and their gods.

There were no rules. Some monsters were up and down holding their plates, and others preferred sitting on the floor as they gratified themselves with different meal courses that were being served. It was not much of a surprise to see many of them frolicking barefoot; they had kicked off their shoes, connecting more with nature – enjoying and absorbing all it had to offer without the hindrance of inevitable obstructions. Most of them had very wide feet and tiny toes that were splay, most probably brought about by them hardly ever wearing shoes. Surely, they never donned shoes that often. If they did, it would be only for special occasions or just for a short time of swanking. Luckily in this instance, all broken pieces of the shattered fan had vanished; a job that had been done by the industrious kitchen team. The monsters were able to soak in a pleasant moment.

The food had also attracted a battalion of hungry bugs. The crawlers moved helter-skelter around plates and spills. Some snoopy ones were tickling the ogres, attempting to climb up their legs. The mammoths now had an extra job to wrestle with, other than eating – swooping off the tiny insects. It did not seem an annoying task to them though, in the face of things; it was part of the deal. The bugs bred and raised their brood freely in the hidden dingy corners of the building.

Seriously, Food-Killer was not in a good mood – she could have at least shared her recipe with the cooks, regardless of being barred from the kitchen. She had done it before for other dishes, on a few previous occasions. On a good day, she would have collected as many of the crawling insects, single-handedly, to cook up a storm – her famous mouth-watering dish, *Sautéed Pimiento Bugs*, which was loved by all. They ate it as snack, enjoying it throughout Boisterous Day or at any other fête. Food-Killer made her own pimiento powder from the lush cherry peppers of Colossus. Nonetheless, the monsters were all content with the scrumptious dishes that had been prepared and were being served. *Who didn't burp?*

"This is a great job done by the Colossus juniors – extra-terrestrial meal! You must be impressed, Food-Killer... oh, you taught them well," Jumbo gushed, almost halfway through his helping. Food-Killer managed a decent smile, moved by Jumbo's overly excited face.

Monster-Pinniped just rolled on the floor, growling and flipping his limbs, not to take care of itchy spots on this occasion, but for tummy satisfaction. His belly was engorged, and the rise and fall of his breathing patterns drew attention. He breathed too heavily, making the involuntary drawing in of oxygen and the discharge of the carbonic acid gas seem an effortful job for one's body. He had eaten various kinds of bird carcasses, his comfort food. Given Boisterous Day, there was a marvellously wide selection, which still left him with no flexible options but to gnaw on everything and bear witness to how each and every presented variety tasted.

Monster Avid-Thwack sat right in the corner as she crunched down beast bones. She picked up more bones from fellow friends around her and worked on them too, unfazed.

"Ah, take it easy, Thwack!" Monster-Monsleek called out. She was following the ogress with her eyes as she left her sitting place to go over to other sections to shovel up some more bones onto her plate. The two were seated together, in the same corner. "Your body needs to recover first," she warned. Unfortunately, it was bouncing onto deaf ears. It was Boisterous Day for Avid-Thwack too, she had to eat! Nothing was going to be of much importance to her, other than grinding the day away.

Food-Killer had tried to be quiet for a reasonable length of time. She however failed abysmally, holding it there to stretch much longer to perhaps the end of the day, without causing a flutter in the dovecote.

"How come I only got three lizards...?" she grumbled, glaring at Monsleek's plate.

"Don't start, Food-Killer. You gobbled up all your snails and frogs and lizards – right before our eyes – and now you want to start... Argh, enough. Don't be silly, argh..." Monster-Monsleek struck back, pouting her face as she tried covering her plate with her hands.

"No, man, Monsleek, why be so grouchy... Let's stop this selfishness!"

"Hey, Starwartle, tell the cooks to bring the whole pot to Food-Killer." That was Johnny-Warlock, all in high spirits as he pranced to music in the background. They had later on adjusted to Monster-Treble's new millennium gadgets.

"Look who's even talking..." Monsleek shook her head in disbelief, darting her eyes at Warlock. She'd anticipated Johnny-Warlock would easily go against Food-Killer, especially after the make-up washing scene. Johnny however, had his own plans brewing in the head.

Just then, another group of ogresses called her to join them where they were sitting. Avid-Thwack clung on to a bead on Monsleek's skirt as soon as she stood up. "No, stay here, Monsleek," she tried to persuade, but Monsleek had already made up her mind.

"You'll break off the bead, Thwack," she complained, pulling her skirt gently, and Avid-Thwack released it immediately. Monsleek walked off with all her belongings.

"I'm watching!" At once, Twelve-eyed Monster' pompous voice bellowed through the microphone. Johnny-Warlock continued dancing as if nothing had happened. He ignored the set of eyes that seemed to be flashing at him. Nothing under the sun was to bring him back from cloud nine. He turned around, flipping his hands up into the air and clicking his fingers simultaneously. His actions attested that Boisterous excitement was fully ignited in him!

Meanwhile, Food-Killer threw one of the three lizards she was left with into her mouth and hid the remaining two underneath some creamy mash on her plate. She subsequently patted the top flat with her blubbery fingers. In her nature, patience was miserably limited. Waiting for the cooks to do another round was more like waiting for a whole new season to crop up. She kept fidgeting as if her seat had prickly bristles, whilst her eyes went on journeying around, plate to plate, assessing other ogres eating patterns. She would most probably chronicle on paper how each and every individual took every bite of their food, including their eating tempos.

All pranks and stories that were turning up around her, were sheer purposeless noise. Food-Killer was wandering in her edgy emotions, which had apparently consumed the better of her. A young monster sitting across from her was fussily mopping up her plate with her fingers. She had bolted down all her food already and seemed to be in preparation for a second round as well.

The greedy giantess Food-Killer almost jumped off her seat when she took notice of one cook walking straight to her. She was to be served first. Her name at the top of the hierarchy for second helpings was huge! A dishing spoon clung by a condor wing on the top part of the cook's apron, bouncing about his chest. It was mystifying how it was able to perch there on a single flat wing without falling.

The cook walked on confidently, like he was under a spell. A rich brown soup had trickled down the sides of the cauldron he was carrying. The pot was completely covered in soot, having been brought straight from the open fire, but the dripping soup stood out still. It claimed the authority to enthral many. Food-Killer locomoted carefree... she could not hide her beaming face. Her eyes looked sunken – submerged by her smiling bouffant cheeks. All was well.

With his lanky torso, Johnny-Warlock leaped up and about, going ahead with dancing. The giant did not seem to care anymore about his facial looks. He had washed himself clean, removing all the greasy soup and residue of the messed-up make-up. He never bothered to go out looking for convenient clay to improvise with.

There he was now – back on the dance floor after the afternoon meal. He was like a kangaroo, hopping freely in a quiet jungle just after rain, opting to forget for at least one moment that poachers existed. Johnny's rollicking demeanour was admired by so many ogres. He always drew attention, every time he rose up to dance.

He kept going...

His hypnotizing moves were so exhilarating that most monsters could not resist joining in, and Freaky-Buddy was the first one to rise. His mysterious monstrous spirits had been provoked, bringing all his energy to life. As soon as he was granted permission, the monster swaggered straight to the platform, going after the trusted wooden floor that did justice to his tap-dancing performances.

Now, with his boisterous moves, especially after the decadent lunch, the floor sounded as if it had gone hollow underneath, and all the sounds were pounding back with force. His feet had turned a little heavier than before. His focus had been lost too. *Doubtless!* To humans it would turn out exasperating but the ogres clapped on – enshrined in a rollicksome bubble.

Lazy monsters had started yawning and stroking their tummies, but the day was not over as yet.

"Is that you?"

"Nope, maybe her."

"Who... me? Not me, it's coming from that side."

"Nay, and your side too – don't deny."

*Random voices projected from different areas in the hall.*

"Ha-ha...ha-ha...ha-ha!" They all laughed away, accusing each other of causing foul smells. Their systems were at serious work. It was Boisterous Day! No average human being would survive the dangerous gases that were expelled inside of Behemoth Hall.

"Water, please. Hey, Starwartle, get us some water to drink!" Monster Fiery-Fireball yelled out, munching his last chunk of the warty goblin pumpkin. His lips were infested with the blazing orange particles of the extraordinary squash. He tipped his head frontward, swallowing it up, as if he was choking on it. "My throat is crackly dry..." he expressed in a congested voice, placing his hand onto his neck. He proceeded giving it a gentle rub with his fingers.

Given her four arms, it surely was an easy task for Starwartle to carry the hugest Behemoth water vessel. It was big enough to quench every monster's thirst. She placed the vessel right in the centre of the hall.

"Uh ha... Good job, little monster..." Fiery-Fireball appreciated, and a loud belch erupted behind his words. As thirsty as he had portrayed himself to be, monster-king, Jack-eyed, was given first priority to drink. He seemed to be virtually back to his senses as he lumbered to the vessel, flexing his muscles. Jack-eyed was full of it – self-pride, absolute lordliness! It appeared to have completely vanished out of him that he had got badly drunk and caused a scene in the earlier hours.

Jack-eyed had shortly returned from the private recovery room where he had been taken to recuperate.

Monster Twelve-eyed drank the water second and Freaky-Buddy went thereafter. Using individual ostrich eggshells, all the other monsters took turns to quench their thirst too.

On his way back from the water vessel, Fiery-Fireball spattered some water onto Monster-Pinniped. He dipped his fingers into his eggshell and sprinkled the driblets straight onto his head. Pinniped winked his slumberous eye in response, followed by a mere grin. He remained lying there on the floor. "*That's what I've been longing for...*" was the image he depicted.

"Get up!" Monster Fiery-Fireball said to Pinniped as he walked away. Pinniped simply rolled over, changing his sleeping position.

"What are you even fighting for?" Fiery curiously enquired as he approached a group of young ogres who were quarrelling in his way.

"Yes, please, Monster Fiery-Ball – can you tell us who invented the art of making shoes," one of them articulated.

"Shoes have always been worn, ever since water was first drunk," Fiery smattered, leaving them all quiet and gaping at one another, wondering. He walked away a bit and then stopped, turning back to them. There was a wide smile on the giant's face. His lips were still invaded by the pumpkin particles – now dried. He took a sip of water out of his container and young ogres laughed away, toddling outside to their own private space.

"Watch it! Watch it!" in no seconds, '...*bash!*' At full throttle, heavy bottoms landed on food, splashing it all around. It was a mind-blowing, shambolic episode. A lot was happening in Behemoth Hall – simultaneously. The wooden platter crashed into numerous bits and a chip sprang across a couple of monsters, and landed up on Monster-Monsleek's plate, which was on her lap.

"Oh no, sorry, I ought to... Uhm, very sorry, whose food was it?" The warning had come a little too late. Monster-Oblivious, Teras dweller, had flumped right onto the food and the platter was apparently hers. The slouchy giant had not been focussing at all when she got back from getting her water. A brief phase of silence followed. The giants sitting in the same space all stared at her. Monster-Oblivious's mind seemed to be meandering astray. She was probably processing what had just happened or it was simply a feeling of trepidation. Her eyes had gone glossy with tears, but just then she roared out a jaw-droppingly thunderous belt of laughter. It dispelled the tinge of humiliation that had started brewing up. As awkward as it was, everyone joined in and they all went hysterical!

Pelting rains, sunshine, drizzle or fog – the apt ones knew it was their special day still and was worthy of not being wasted. It was Boisterous!

Sluggish and forgetful was Monster-Oblivious. Nevertheless, she was well accepted by all in her community.

On the other end, Monster-Monsleek – all illuminated – continued slitting into her chunks of meat and churning them with her small but proficient teeth – unaware of any intrusions onto her plate by whatsoever foreign particles. To all appearances, every bite was tasty, which was amplified by her trade of dishing out other ogresses' dirt.

She was sitting with a Teras ogre who was also absorbed into the conversation. He had installed himself right on the table, hunched over, facing Monsleek, who was on the chair. He picked up a piece of meat from Monsleek's plate on the spur of the moment and did not appear to have noticed anything odd on the platter either. He teased Monsleek with the meat – drawing it back and forth from her lips a couple of times, like he intended to feed her. He then popped it into his mouth, laughing. Monsleek kicked him lightly on the shin with a gleeful chuckle. The two were in their own bubble, enjoying each other's company.

# 12

Finally, the Boisterous Foot Race they always anticipated on the special day could now start.

Jack-eyed was now fully back at the helm as the master of ceremonies. In no good minutes after he announced the kick off of the race, most monsters had flocked to both doorways, squeezing to go outside. This made going out a snail pace process. Monster-Jumbo was one of the first individuals to rise. The group used the larger exit. This time around Jumbo confidently employed his earlier trick of success and it took him much less time to execute.

After roughly twenty minutes, the main exit went quiet. All remaining monsters who were still inside had clumped at the second door, which was much smaller.

"Ah-aah...h-e-l-p... ouch! My back...ow..." In a short order, Monster Fiery-Fireball cried out, pleading from a different end. He slipped – falling at breakneck speed onto the hard, concrete floor! Yes, it was a very bad fall. Clearly, in his mind he had synthesised that he was being clever, avoiding the stampede that had built up at the smaller exit. He had initially stood there for a few minutes, right at the back of the multitude, before walking off to the other door. Little had he known that the ogres who went in through the larger way out earlier had wickedly squashed all the unwanted fruit and banana peels onto the hallway floor leading outside. Fireball only saw the muddle when he got right there; it was a bit late to turn back. Nonetheless, he literally never appeared to have made any great deal out of it.

He continued groaning, holding his back, sitting there on the floor, but nobody seemed to care. Laughing at him was simply a way of begging for fireballs, so nobody attempted it. They had to consequently bite their tongues. Out of frustration, Monster Fiery-Fireball removed all the mash stuck onto his feet and smeared it right onto the wall. He got up, determined to look out for his close pal. Luckily, there was a spyhole right above him; he thrust his eye searching outside. All he wanted was pity and mercy. Jack-eyed was a great pacifier!

The furry mammoth realised King Jack-eyed was very busy outside. He was fighting his own battle. He had an obligation to impress and prove to all the giants that he was now in a very sound condition, and in full control. He had to justify his occupation of the pinnacle position – Colossus King.

"Argh, I don't care. I'm still going to win the race and right in their faces I'll show them!" Fiery-Fireball muttered, comforting himself. He shook himself and in no time he had joined others alfresco – ready to propel.

Their starting point was the corner of Ogre Street, right next to the Behemoth enclosure. It was just four steps away from the gate for most monsters.

"Where is Food-Killer?" one monster enquired, looking around, confused. She could not be spotted anywhere in the vicinity of the racing point.

The monster head cook had fallen asleep on the steps by the lavatory entrance. Few giants had seen her. She was awkwardly slumped in a heap, most probably tired after the nasty chase. She was all covered by the heavy cloak. Although she was doubtlessly under intense heat, Food-Killer seemed at peace, enjoying her sleep, and she remained there – snoring and snoring with not the slightest shift in sleeping position. Fellow monsters did not attempt to wake her. They knew she was not going to make it to the race by any chance. Despite the chase, she had been caught ravishing a half-potful of mushrooms behind the kitchen storeroom door. She had got away with it. It wasn't reported to higher authorities.

Nevertheless, the race went ahead. It was a very long and tiresome distance. It took two good hours for the first monster to return. Surely, an ordinary human mind would have thought of the worst – earth tremor – as the indefinite number of heavy-footed mammals pounded the land surface, all of them aiming for front positions!

All roads leading into the kingdom of Arcane were jammed by the participating runners. They had to reach the centre of the capital city, and at a specified rockery had to pull off a monster flag each and take it back to their starting point at Behemoth. The flags were red and white. Imprinted on them were faces of their fallen ogre heroes.

As the very special guest, Monster Freaky-Buddy, the Teras king, stayed at the hall. He cheerfully welcomed back the participants upon their return. Indeed, it had happened. In accordance with his expectations and with what his name entailed; the obnoxious Fiery-Fireball was in the lead – second to none. He was absolutely fleet-footed! Ghost-Hound, the repulsive spiny-skinned monster, was in second place and immediately after him was famous Monster-Monsleek. Not according to his plans and wishes, Johnny-Warlock fell in the fourth position, tying with Jumbo. Although the largest, and having the widest foot span in the crowd, Monster-Jumbo's physique did not allow him to propel that fast. He was, however, ecstatic at representing the Teras community in a top-five position.

All the other monsters came after randomly. There were a lot more ties too, other than Jumbo and Warlock's. Second from last was Starwartle. Everyone had anticipated at least the second place for her, since she was the youngest participant and presumably the healthiest. Alas, it was not the year and day for her. She had also been weighed down by the immense stress and pressure she had undergone earlier on in the day.

Much later, when everyone else was cooling off, Pinniped appeared from down the hill. He was all fatigued, but still, with two flags tightly tucked under his flipper arms, he kept at it –

tottering up the hill, striving to reach the finish line. His folks laughed and exhorted him all at once, as they watched him use up his final burst of energy. Having taken stopovers along the way, Monster-Pinniped had delayed himself and that reserved for him the last position. He had taken a plunge into Terror Ditch twice – on the way to and back – to re-energise.

Terror Ditch was just outside Colossus kingdom, before crossing over into Arcane. The ditch was very deep and fairly wide. It held slimy green water, which was cryptic and seemed to be a roof, concealing a whole lot of dark activities beneath. There were always clots of evil-looking auburn masses afloat on the water. The masses had numerous cilium type of hairs around them, which endowed them with the privilege of drifting about freely. Sight of the pool isunnerving to a moderate mind – a glance of it quickly sends terrifying signals through the system, alarming the body to prepare for what could be a clan of vampires almost, or perhaps rising then and there, forthwith, from the subsurface.

Terror Ditch had also become a final resting place for many kinds of insects and arthropods. Pinniped's plunge into the pool had stirred about their rise from the bottom, together with a sludge of mud and decayed vegetation. The lot concocted with the rest of the water, which further thickened it temporarily. The close-by Dragon Tree, elevating its crown above the pool, offered decent shade protection, which partially contributed to the maintenance of coolness of the green waters, day and night. The Dragon Tree had grotesque tumours of blood throughout its trunk that stood like a testimony to working tirelessly, fighting some secret sacred wars. The trunk cracked at timely intervals, causing its fibres to bleed profusely for a moment. They would then dry up in preparation for another. Boisterous Day had met up with one of its surliest days of spurting!

# 13

A couple of hours later, Food-Killer finally woke up and her face was drenched with sweat. Straight from her sleep – although disoriented and panicky – she was still able to carry herself with vigour. She ran around flaunting some win of a particular medal! 'Supreme Racer...' It was jaw-dropping to everyone there, but they all remained mum. Her cloak was in her hands; it was safer there... reckoning the way she was swamped in a delirium of celebrating her Boisterous Day achievement!

"I knew you were not ever going to catch up with my speed, Warlock," she said, brushing her shoulder against him.

"H'm," Johnny-Warlock lazily uttered and the conversation died instantly. He simply threw vacant stares at her.

Post-haste, the 'Supreme Racer' award winner headed to the kitchen. She appeared to have been dissatisfied with Warlock's reactions. In no seconds she cannonballed back outside. She appeared pitiably aggrieved; a sudden and complete metamorphosis of her earlier mood. Her brows were tightly furrowed, and her body looked tense.

Swiftly – she exploded!

"Who took my medal?"

"Huh-huh?"

Her eyes intently searched for answers from the onlookers. "Somehow, I knew this would happen. Now, tell me, who has it?" She kept probing for the *'oh, it's here'* answer, which never surfaced. She glowered at Johnny-Warlock, who simply glowered back in return. Silent.

"Don't stare at me like that! I'm not a large block of food!" Food-Killer went berserk.

Everybody was stunned. She stood there with her hands akimbo, jiggling one leg, and the stumpy tail went rigidly straight, in synergy with her eccentric act. "Do I look like *Achatina carcass?* Come on, put me in the pot then. Make sure you add enough seasoning," she bleated on, blinking her eyes manifold times a minute.

"Who stole it? I left my med–" she stuttered with rage.

She slid fingers into her hair and pulled it really hard, like she intended to uproot it all. Sweat and tears trickled profusely from the anxious monster. She turned around and around on the same spot, and later tilted her head, looking up to the sky. It were as if she expected to find the medal floating down on a tray, being returned to her from another planet in the celestial realm.

"I'm simply asking who stole my trophy from the kitchen counter?" she then said, reiterating for the billionth time, her voice quadruple times higher. Stretching to half an hour, the female mammoth continued foaming at the mouth, throwing tantrums. She was surely up to causing trouble – serious trouble, one more time before the sun slipped into the horizon. She posed so ready, appearing all pumped up to jump onto somebody's throat.

"Okay, okay, please shush, everyone! Johnny-Warlock cut in. "Lend me your ears for a second, Food-Killer – where is your flag? Just show us your flag and please explain to us what happened along the way to Arcane." He had finally harnessed the courage to stand up against her, knocking her over with a feather. His hands were knotted behind his back as he looked intently at her. Food-Killer fell into perplexity mode in a flash and had nothing to say.

"Look folks, *hahaha!* It's coming out. Just a bee in her hat. We haven't even received the awards as yet."

"Which world are you in, Food-Killer?" Monster Johnny-Warlock dissected her senses. "You're only 'Supreme Racer' perhaps when it comes to fleeing with food, and for that, yes – we salute you!"

Although seething, other monsters simply sat back, gaping at the unfolding bizarre scene. They simply did not want to intensify the situation after such an awesome race. Nobody was prepared to lose their toes, after all. Food-Killer's flare-up was left with no room to bloom any further. She had been lucky that the leaders had gone in for yet another quick meeting, and to fetch the medals.

Although beset by a tinge of disappointment, Food-Killer finally came to cognition and accepted that the 'Supreme Racer' medal had just been a fantasy in her shut-eye moment. She was somewhat consoled when Pinniped sincerely gave her one of the monster flags he had plucked. She was tickled pink – her lashes were fluttering mildly like those of a doll. She re-donned her cloak and waved the flag around with a winsome smile.

# 14

They quickly brushed aside all their disputes and settled down for dessert. Hunky-dory moment was manifested – filling the atmosphere. The afters were generously served outside. The wind was breathing moderately through the lavish green, and the long grass waggled and whistled profusely in response, whilst the verdant leaves kept fluttering, lustrously beautiful, up on the trees. The leaves deflected sun rays at frequent intervals, which created sporadic ghostly shadows around the space. The sun was now melting away from bright yellow to a milder golden colour. Dead leaves on the top layer were being continuously swept gently on the ground – forming scenic waves that were accompanied by a graceful rustling sound.

The food was dished onto their customary carved wooden platters, and all portions were monolithic. It was Boisterous Day! A second barrel of juice had been brought outside too. All monsters were taking regular visits to the station, refilling their empties.

"This juice earnestly deserves a special name of its own," Twelve-eyed proposed, looking carefully at the crimson-coloured beverage in his adorned ostrich eggshell – their drinking containers.

"Hey-hey, cheers to that!" His sentiment was backed up by King Jack-eyed, without any reservations. They both raised their drinks in honour. A combination of berries and bush cherries had created magic. The two leaders did not shy away either, going for more and more, together with everyone else. Jack-eyed now stirred away completely from the enchanted, trouble-causing fermented drink!

All monsters' faces shone bright, revealing their buoyant spirits. They mingled more, and their voices got louder and louder. A mountainous swarm of caterpillars was magically turned into a fancy compote by the cooks. They mixed in lots of nuts, and the dish was accompanied by some sacred kind of honey. The honey was unique – very dark and gooey, and jiggly all at once. It was highly valued in this vibrant community.

Of course, wild fruits were there too, and were presented separately. Batches were sorted according to their types and it showed off their clear-cut colours – some were green, others purple. Yellow was there too, and brown, which was the largest heap and held numerous variations that many preferred. Fresh berries were mixed with honey and whey.

They made their own whey, which was another process that was done few days prior to Boisterous. They prepared it by curdling milk, then separating the curds from the colourless liquid. The filtered curds were salted and further used for other foodstuffs, including farmer's cheese, whilst the whey went to cater for dessert.

Whatever they felt like having from the list of the dessert selection was up to individual choices – they were being spoilt on their special day.

One monster-cook appeared outside holding a mega bucket of ice-cream, all exposed to the heat of the late afternoon.

It was Ember – the Frog barbecue master!

"*Humph... Whoa...whoa!*"

Before he even got too close to the crowd, the most popular and domineering voice clamoured from behind him. It made him halt instantly.

"What's that you've brought out, young monster? In such broad day light? From where is it sprouting?" the now sober and robust King Jack-eyed queried, and his facial expressions were very apprehensive. The ice-cream was heaped up to the top, and it clearly showed it was not any of their usual staples. It was far away from their cheese – neither was it plain nor jiggly to resemble freshly coagulated milk. Its colour was suspiciously eye-catching... RED. It would surely require more than brawny backbone to convince the monster-king it was safe, as he had right away deemed it strange and possibly a danger.

Others did not receive the meltdown well and all happiness plummeted in seconds. To be interrupted from their ecstatic moment yet again, for the fourth, fifth or sixth time – was an immense insult. They grumbled. They could not clearly count the number of times anymore, neither the sequence of the occurrences. It was more of a pain with no possible cure, according to them. Guttural voices of discomfort reverberated in all areas of the huge crowd.

"Oh, this is called ice-cream, just a dessert. You'll love it, and everybody will, I'm pretty sure. It's scrummy." Monster-Ember didn't waste any seconds explaining himself in anticipation of a quick approval.

A moment of infrangible quietness crept up immediately after his words. It was still a long way to being vindicated, if he ever were to be, the youngster realised.

Jack-eyed seemed as though he was dissecting each and every word that had hit his eardrums... thoroughly examining the whole string before responding or casting an action. He was mildly shaking his head. Nobody would dare utter a word to interrupt the mute process, but the young ogre cook did.

"We made it ourselves in the kitchen, just a borrowed formula... liked a lot by humans. It's as sweet as our ambrosia honey." Ember jabbered away confidently, showing no signs of being shaken. The bucket appeared dead mass heavy; his shoulders were slanted at an angle.

"What?" the Colossus king snarled. The young monster was taken aback. "Our Boisterous Day is being ruined here, messed up in a very dangerous manner!" Jack-eyed huffed. The young giant's response had surely fallen short of convincing the strict monster leader.

Jack-eyed's shock and anger forced him to push away the platter that was in front of him. It held his favourite *palate cleanser* meal. He had been peacefully savouring every bite of it – fresh hands of ginger, with honey dolloped on the side as a dip.

He slapped the sides of his thighs lightly with open hands – five times, rapidly, as if he was out of ideas and did not know what to do next. Then he suddenly dropped one side of his spectacles. They never fell off completely; the one side went dangling as he repositioned himself to face Ember squarely. He jutted out his chin, narrowing the naked eye, and sternly switched focus – ping-ponging between the ice-cream bucket and the junior ogre bearing it. He subsequently shut both his eyes and paused for a little while, breathing in deeply, trying hard to snuff out his anger. He then continued as calmly as he could.

"What's the point here? I don't understand; what's the point? You say the ice-cream tastes like our ambrosia honey – so we'll just eat our customary honey then. Given caterpillars on the side, an additional flourish... won't that be more than adequate? Why would we sacrifice our eternity for the satisfaction of just a minute?" he boldly questioned, disparaging all the earlier points that had been given. His eyes were probing Ember's face, expecting his lips to formulate only lucid answers.

"What gives it the colour of blood then – grumous tears of the Dragon's Tree, right?" Jack-eyed quickly posed yet another question.

"No-no-no, it's simply beetroot that painted it," Ember responded speedily.

"I still fail to understand. We have beets on our plates here – a whole wide variety of roots, and I'm having ginger!" He pointed at his platter. "What is wrong with eating the actual beetroot, in its purest form?" he asked.

"You're hiding something from me, young monster. There's something you're holding back; I can feel it."

To an extent, Jack-eyed had simmered down. Nonetheless, his approach to solving issues was slightly different from Twelve-eyed's. Yes, King Jack-eyed was viewed as just as strict, but his pride and passion were mainly to protect rather than causing harm unnecessarily, or flaunting. Twelve-eyed was conceited. He craved to be feared, and all other things fell at the bottom of his list. Ruling was simply a moment of having supreme powers, so he perceived.

"Umm, well... thought we could just give it a try, my King". Under his breath, Monster-Ember persisted one more time. What he was anchoring on, only the gods knew.

King Jack-eyed could not believe his ears. "Absurd!" he lambasted and stood up right away. He thumped over to where the monster-cook was standing. "My ears desire to hear nothing more from you, Ember! Enough – enough – enough! I mean enough!"

It jolted a slew of ogres. They chuntered in dampened voices. Ember remained there; he never attempted to move. It would possibly aggravate the situation, and that he knew.

Monster Freaky-Buddy was shocked too. He was freaking out, fearing the worst.

"What a blow... What has got into our young monsters?" he blustered, rubbing his palms desperately – clearly broadcasting his worries. "It's the same back in Teras. The number of young hopefuls is dwindling if we don't act."

His feelings were overt. He looked at his fellows' reactions and found it unsurprising that they were mirroring his own.

"Sad," he let out the simple yet hefty word in an undertone.

Monster-Ember, now cowering and with all the radiance on his face withering, realised he had initiated a dreadful mistake. The Colossus monster-king was well known; he was invincible, especially when it came to their eating tradition. He was very tenacious.

The king glared down at him like he was about to toss him into the air, or split his nose open! "Come on, Ember, drop that barrel and go on your botties. You must always sit when being reprimanded. Have you forgotten primal rules?" the Teras king intervened, trying to cushion the situation before it escalated too severely.

"*Ewwww,* Monster Freaky-Buddy stop! *Holier-than-thou...* Were you not fighting just few hours ago? We're not even talking of a week past... have you forgotten?" Avid-Thwack ambushed the Teras ruler and got everyone easing up for a moment.

"*It's a funny old-world, ha!"* he responded.

"I was simply defending myself that time. I got trapped. Come on folks. You got to be kidding me," Freaky-Buddy spurted, sounding exasperated. His aim was to get his name cleansed before leaving the powerful kingdom, but the turn in the direction of things did not seem to be favouring his interests.

"Naked truth you've been told, *ha*?" Food-Killer would not have let the ongoing scene slip by without twitting either. Freaky chose to remain quiet, or perhaps he had simply run out of words.

"See, clammed up! The orange ball in the sky has split into two... we all can see," Food-Killer snorted – prompting a young ogress who was sitting in the parallel aisle to go manic, convulsing with laughter. She unfortunately made a spectacle of herself, which in turn provided a welcome breather for Ember. Despite laughing out the loudest – above everyone else – the young ogress was completely clueless that she was spilling the whey dessert she was holding. Her other hand was endlessly stirring the overly filled up drink with a long stem, which had a fat berry hanging at the bottom. For almost three minutes, she went on oscillating the berry stem, like a pendulum – while convulsing – until the voice of Avid-Thwack chided her!

"What if your future husband is here in the crowd?"

Avid-Thwack went on to grasp the busy arm by the elbow, running her eyes over the junior ogress, examining her from head to toe, as if her perfect body had transformed into a feathered tree. The young damsel immediately shut her mouth and calmed down, but Thwack's grip remained firmly affixed onto the poor arm, burrowing her fingers into the flesh and making her sizz.

"Release her, Avid!" Jack-eyed commanded from where he was standing, grilling Ember. The female mammoth gave a timid smile and obeyed. She went on to wrap her arms around the young ogress's body, bringing her closer to her chest – squeezing her hard like a python, incapacitating her upper limbs, as if to say sorry for the earlier lashing out. Her teeth were right on the youngster's forehead.

The young ogress managed to safely wriggle out of the strange bonds in not much time. Avid-Thwack scoffed at the episode with her head lowered. She adjusted the sleeve of her blouse that was rolled up, before straightening out her Payara fangs' brooch that too had gone askew. The young ogress meanwhile shook herself with great relief and reached for her dessert that she had placed down in fear. Her facial looks were confusing – half nervous, and the other fraction seemingly triumphant. There were light impressions of Thwack's two front teeth on her forehead.

"That wasn't impressive, Avid-Thwack," a throaty, raspy voice startled the two. The ogress in a choking ghoulish ash-grey train dress appeared right in front of the two, who were both in a semi-conscious abyss of their own. She gracefully extended her arm, taking the young ogress by her hand, and waddled away with her to a different sitting area. Thwack was left cracking her knuckles, looking dazed.

"Bring over a basin of meat, *err...* someone. Avid needs to busy herself here – that's all," said Fiery, suggesting the best therapy for his acquaintance.

Everything unfolded in unbelievably non-major bits... A wooden basin that closely resembled the carapace of a leopard tortoise was availed to Thwack, within the same window. It was chock-full.

Thereafter, all eyes lurched back to Monster-Ember, who had already dropped the *evil* barrel.

He was hunkered on his heels initially, displaying childish emotions of protest. He was a minor still though, at the bodily size of just below an average human being. He was about 65 inches.

After a short while, without anybody's word, he slid off gently from the dusty soles of his shoes and sat as advised. He placed his elbows onto his knees and clasped his hands together. There was a visible fresh blister on the side of his right hand; a tattoo of working extra hard in the kitchen, endorsed on him by none other than piping hot liquid.

Jack-eyed clucked before giving tongue to his inner feelings once more. He looked at the ice-cream very carefully, stroking his chin. His body language clearly spelt the words **'completely disapproved'** – in bold.

"This new generation of ours... coming up at their own terms. It's a pity, really," and again, he clucked. "It's possibly caused by consumption... noshing these weird, unknown foreign victuals." He was less agitated, which gave relief to everybody. He flashed his eyes onto the small soft pocket of fluid puffed up on the young cook's hand, and promptly shifted to his dismayed face.

"Now, look here, pay close attention..." Jack-eyed stressed. "If I may explain to you, in case you haven't heard or haven't known... whatever! We monsters don't do that; we never attempt. I don't know how many times I'd have to emphasise this: there's no way we can ever play dangerously – eating stuff that might drain us of our powers! *What deliberate stupidity would that be?* Turn ourselves sensitive and fragile and feeble or the worst – pea size... *Knowingly?*" He gave out a clamorous exhale. It left the attendees a bit churned up. They knew it was going to consume a huge segment of their glee time, much more than they had calculated.

King Jack-eyed hurled his eyes back at the unwanted tin before turning his attention to the monster-gatherers. He took another deep breath. It must have been the furthest his diaphragm had ever expanded.

"Who pictures themselves basking amongst a flock of Zombies here?" he later asked, skimming around as if he seriously anticipated a 'yes' response from any member.

"Now, take heed everybody," he asserted in a draconian manner, with hands throwing metaphoric gestures simultaneously. "I don't tolerate such negligence. No-no-no-never! We only touch foods of the gods; the only stuff that the majority of humans respect by shying away from. Exclusive, nothing less... that's what we consume."

He finally ripped off his spectacles. Holding them in one hand, he wiped his face with the other. It was as if he were rinsing off the anger that had unfurled in him, or he was perhaps trying to come to terms with the reality that was set before his eyes.

He continued. It wasn't over yet... "You can sulk – whine – it's okay, hey, little one. At least it'll be for an hour or two – I don't care – but your future will be protected. You must plead for forgiveness later at the sacrifice altar. Now, away you go at once!"

He sealed off his rage that had been burning like wildfire by pointing in the direction of the Behemoth kitchen. His arm was quivering to the same beat as the nerves pulsating on the sides of his head. Monster-Ember managed a slight nod of remorse and wistfully scurried back, holding his ice-cream, to where Jack-eyed's finger pointed.

"Like our condor...!" Jack-eyed bawled, and all monsters articulated back with vigour, finishing off their slogan. "... Fearless we unfurl and soar!"

"How I wish Jack-eyed had given me the opportunity to deal with that one. I bet I'd have done far better than the sluggishness he showed us," Twelve-eyed grumbled, gritting his teeth, throwing unreadable gestures with all his four arms. He was conversing with ogres who were sitting adjacent to him.

"Why don't you just wait for the vote-counting hour, then you freely execute all that your heart deems so necessary?" one ogre hurled at him, all soaked up with anger. The giants did not seem excited about engaging on the matter any further with Twelve-eyed – but he seemed keyed-up to cast an action. He went on maundering to himself. The other ogre's words could have also grazed his ego; he shot him such a dirty look, and the ogre glowered back.

But the celebrations had to continue! The day was surely treading to an end and they had to make the best of the remaining hours.

# 15

A little later, Food-Killer sneaked into the kitchen, taking advantage of the favourable circumstances at hand. Celebratory momentum had built up outside. In that hour, it appeared no one was conscious of her once again devil-may-care actions.

She shut the door behind her.

"*Shik-shik-sha...* I'll break the rules tonight!" the plump mammoth declared to herself in a guttural voice whilst scouting all directions. The kitchen was quiet, which encouraged her crazy demeanour.

Quickly, she spotted the controversial vessel. "This day only comes once every 365 days. I've been quiet, very silent for hours – if Jack-eyed's glasses are transparent enough, am sure he saw it too. I DESERVE a reward." She cemented her ludicrous plan as she headed straight for the ice-cream.

She swigged down a great many gallons. Her adam's apple reported a deliciously smooth job as it maintained a steady rhythm of swallowing. It showed the ice-cream was all melted.

She almost got carried away, forgetting that she was breaking extremely serious rules, but luck seemed to be on her side still.

Eventually, she placed it down, trying to catch a breath. She lodged her elbows firmly onto the table and leaned over, looking at the pleasant frothy red liquid, as if she was kowtowing to it. Her breath was hiccupy.

"They must confess to me how they created this..." she said ultimately, in a thickly tremulous voice. A significant amount of creamy foam was dripping down her chin, but she didn't get a chance to wipe it off. There was absolutely no time set aside for that. It further dropped – finding haven on her clothes. Her tongue had only managed a partial licking job, as she rose up walking towards the storeroom. She wasn't as gifted as many of her folks who had much larger tongues.

She squatted, picking up an empty wooden keg of ambrosia honey to utilize for her sweet takeaway. The keg had been abandoned by the storeroom door. The ogress seemed to be striking gold all the way!

She wouldn't have dared to leave the ice-cream and ever be at peace beyond Boisterous Day.

She walked in a bit farther and cast a sinister look into the storeroom. She frowned. There was nothing delicious to appreciate out of the scatter that was virtually claiming up all the space. It was rather overwhelming. Her baskets of herbs and spices seemed to have had fallen off the shelves, and the dispelled packages added to the slew of haphazardness that lay on the floor.

Just before she stepped back into the kitchen, she stopped abruptly. She stood still – trying to follow some movements with her ears. There was a loud noise of fast-approaching foot stamps just outside in the passageway. Her back went flat against the storeroom entrance way, and she held the empty keg really tight in her arms. She shut her eyes, waiting for the unknown to explode. In a snap, somebody pushed the kitchen door slightly open – revealing only a partial side of face, and asymmetrical fingertips that gripped onto the side of the door.

"Anybody there?" the disembodied voice enquired, and the front part of a shoe popped into view. It could have been anyone; many ogres had a similar kind of footwear and bodily features.

Food-Killer remained silent on her spot, suppressing her breath. She had to. Getting caught would conceivably mean disaster. She was most likely conversing with her core thoughts in the moment – engineering a next move to escape the cloudy moment that had just befallen.

To her surprise, the door was immediately closed – with a bang – and silence quickly prevailed. She was vastly astounded!

The female mammoth hurriedly stepped back into the kitchen. She decked the keg onto the table, and proceeded to attend to the ultra-crucial task at hand... She shot to the *dangerous* door and latched it with vigour, then turned to the other one, leading outside, and did the same fix! The entire space was now hers. It appeared not to have crossed her mind to have done it at the outset. Now, she only had to avoid the angles that lay parallel to the kitchen window – the apparently only window available at Behemoth. The encounter had also come as a tell-tale reminder that she needed to not be there in the kitchen for any much longer.

Continuing with her main mission, she carefully decanted the remainder of the ice-cream into the empty dinky barrel. *Voila!* She stooped down to examine what the first drum of food held. Her forehead was perspiring. She was at work. It didn't take any meaningful count of seconds before the giantess dropped the lid back. The drum had a leftover mix of roots, leaves and twigs; drowned in broth, and the leaves were all wilted. Only roots of devil's claw plants agreed with her taste buds, but she didn't pick any... *"Is this what I showed them? Pouring in a whole metric tank of water?"* she muttered, striking the drum with her foot.

The ogress had to quickly compose herself – the drum that was behind was carrying all the leftover meat! It was a collection of various kinds of cuts, of different animals. With her face all lit up, she collected as much as she could, filling up a large, lined bag with mostly bonny chunks. Before placing the lid, she fished out a long neck – *S*-shaped – with her fingertips. It was well dunked in soup. She straight away jostled it into her cheek! It was a pleasurable moment for Food-Killer, gratifying her cravings. She behaved as if she were famished and had not had sight of food in weeks.

Happily, she moved on to assembling all other bits and pieces she had envied throughout the day.

'Get while the getting is still good.' Finally, the wise words struck her.

The monster-cook did security checks again, peeking at the window. Everything seemed to be in order, and she stayed calm. She bundled everything up into a single bale, ready to be taken to a safe hiding place. "I'll face the consequences myself if anything goes amiss. *Turn into a Zombie;* what? Argh... I'm Food-Killer. It's the same rules they've been reciting since ancient days. I don't tremble easily, it's medieval," she grumbled egoistically. "Wednesday, Saturday, Tuesday, or Friday... Friday – argh whatever day... Monday, I'll deal with it the 'F D K' way when it comes. It wags to my tune... oh, that – I'll keep any eye." She rolled her eyes, as if Jack-eyed was there in physical presence, watching her swear.

Exiting through the back door was one of the final pieces to her sly puzzle. She took the bale outside and left it anchored against the wall on the stoop. The other door had to be unlatched before leaving – she had been clever indeed. Just at the time she slid the hook, Monster Fiery-Fireball barged in!

"Oh, you're back in the kitchen, Food-Killer? I need another barrel of juice!" He was stunned to have seen her, but it showed he didn't have much time at his disposal to grill her with any questions. Food-Killer threw her right hand out, showing him the way to the storeroom. He went, lifted the barrel and left. It was the last one available.

*"Whew!"* The giantess was relieved. It shot her optimism really high! Everything seemed ROSY!

On walking back outside, she simply left both doors closed.

After surveying the area, she hefted her bale and stealthily crept away, advancing into the backyard. She rumbled, lurching about with her ginormous load as she disappeared behind, to the other side of the building. The giantess looked certain of where she was headed – her face showed an absolute trust in her preferred hiding location.

She walked straight into the nearby bush. There were many shrubs around and a few scattered huge trees, and the grass was very long. The place was not too far away from Behemoth Hall.

Just as she crossed into the area, her roving eyes were greeted by a sack that appeared like a hummock. It lay a little distant from the skimpy pathway. The sack was partially obscured by a few shrubs, but it clearly looked huge. Oh, Food-Killer had to get to it.

She kicked it lightly. It had movable contents. She had boldness; without giving it much thought, she placed her load down and opened the sack slightly – peeping inside.

"Oh, gosh, no... *Who does this?*" she pitied at a glimpse the contents. There were a couple of knobbly bulbous roots and dozens of carambolas. She speedily tied it and whatever lay beneath back up. Her eyes had seen enough. Her own business had to be taken care of too.

Upon lifting her head, she was face to face with swivelling eyeballs. It was a chameleon. It was roosting on a stump of a felled tree. Its tail was coiled up into a neat pinwheel, and the eyes were busy gallivanting. The special lizard had already stolen the colours on Food-Killer's cloak.

"Hmmm... rubbernecking at me. You aren't a snitch, right?" Food-Killer satirized, looking at the replica colours of her popular garment. She took no further time getting mesmerised, and walked slightly farther into the bush, fearless and happy.

"I'm not the only crafty one it seems – but that tonne of carambolas, though..." She stuck her tongue out. "Let nobody throw their pile on top of mine or anywhere too close." It was perhaps a prayer, as she had reached her destination point. Silence never resonated with Food-Killer. She schlepped the bale, threshing about in the long grass, to rest it right under some umbrella-shaped shrubs. In haste, her mission was done, and she got on her way back to the hall. "If my bulk disappears..." She ended there and gave a maniacal laugh. She was almost stepping out of the wild.

On the spur of the moment, she threw her eyes back into the woods – responding to the prompt of some weird noise! It sounded like a falling tree or something close. She was dismayed.

She stood there, examining closely, trying to register what was happening. It had become too dark for a proper distant focus. There was a figure that fairly resembled that of a mammoth on one of the trees. It just stood out. She zoomed in.

The body did not move, and she didn't either. She tilted her head to all sides, trying to conceptualise. It was just laying still on a bough of the tree. She had walked past the same tree to and fro from her place of privacy. She had seen nothing. There was a clear distinction that it was not a part of the tree. The figure had what looked like a series pattern of horny plates.

"Crocodile loafing... Damn!"

Food-Killer cursed after a moment and walked away. Part of the structure passably resembled a large reptile tail. The spring in her step showed immense relief; a presumption that nobody had caught her in the off-kilter act.

"After all, there're no humans anywhere around here, *hahaha* - they've become clever nowadays... waaaaay clever. He's gonna starve to death nestling in that tree, unless he feeds on grass." She ridiculed the intruder, ironing down her cloak using her hands whilst walking.

"My baggage contains only cooked meat; spiced too... sluggish long lizard." She snapped her fingers three times.

"*Oi!* ... and ice-cream!"

Only after the moment she stated this did she turn her head cursorily toward the woods. She emitted a fruity chuckle thereafter, as she walked on. F D K had guts; she'd been almost reaching the hall entrance by then.

The female mammoth finally stepped back inside Behemoth, and quickly sat with fellow ogresses!

'*Prattle-prattle-prattle*' she gabbed, stealthily interweaving into an ongoing conversation. She coerced herself into promptly feeling comfortable and pretended that she had innocently returned from visiting the lavatory, as she advised when she'd risen from her seat. She had not realised she was harbouring dubious elements. Monster-Oblivious kept throwing her eyes suspiciously at the fresh stains that were sticking out on Food-Killer's clothes, but did not utter a word.

Food-Killer noticed. She checked herself, and promptly disregarded the stance that was most likely to flare up. "Don't allow your excitement to fade out your manners. You're fortunate to be here, Obliv," she warned the Teras giantess, with her eyes thrust onto a mound of well-cleaned up fruit pips, laying bare on Monster-Oblivious's platter.

*"Some more chokecherries?"* she teased her. "I even seconded your name for the special invite you got." Food-Killer signed off with the gentle reminder. She gave the idea that those were the sweetest words to hit their guest's ears with, as depicted by the wide smile that was colourfully planted on her face.

Food-Killer's wisecracking game could have worked in her favour in that particular moment, but Monster-Oblivious discounted the move as being another hour of her ludicrousness. She twisted her lips in distaste. The Teras giantess had hesitated all along earlier on, but only gained confidence this time around to pick some thickly intertwined loops of cobwebs that were attached to Food-Killer's cloak, right behind her left shoulder. The webs were contrasting greatly with the rest of her cloak, worse than the food stains showed. Oblivious placed the 'shady sticky lot' onto Food-Killer's lap – quietly. Food-Killer flinched, but hastily removed it – quietly too.

No one else picked up on the scuffle. It all conformed with Food-Killer's cunning behaviour. Monster-Oblivious's friends were meanwhile pecking her arm, drawing her attention and asking her to give her views on what they were discussing.

She later on turned to them. "What folks? Who did what again...? Do you mean Ghost-Hound, for real?" She had managed to pick up a glimpse of the story at hand amidst her sticky encounter with Food-Killer. They were talking about the time Avid-Thwack fainted earlier in the day.

"I wasn't there though, in the chase, but I heard it was Johnny-Warlock who snatched meat from Avid-Thwack, and she passed out. He must have bashed her in the process. I mean... she can't worship meat to the degree of zonking out," Oblivious went on.

"Yep! That has to be Warlock. That ogre is unhinged," Food-Killer remarked. They all dissolved into laughter.

"Oh, look at him, Johnny-Warlock, I think he heard me." Food-Killer espied and ruptured again. "His warts are dreadful, though, just take a good look... I bet goblins get to swing on them every night," she said and went on cackling for a while.

"So, where did it happen – the whole grab... bash... zonking out thing?" With watery eyes, Food-Killer eventually enquired but she realised she had been left in it all alone. The subject had already shifted to something else.

# 16

The wind of the early evening blew swiftly as the monsters continued relishing their dessert. It was a very splendid way for them to cool down following the ice-cream fracas.

It did not take long before the birds – many of them – began cheeping *'we're back home'* melodies, and the larger ones batted their wings clamorously, like they were in celebration of the big day together with the monsters!

It was that time of the day... Ravens flew into the yard, clasping food in their claws to provide for their young ones back at the nests, and a convocation of eagles also appeared consecutively; heading to their own aeries around the Behemoth wall. Other birds were simply dancing, hanging about in the air – flocking high up in coordinated moves – and flying back fleetly to lower ground, codifying different shapes of the alphabet – perhaps spelling out the name 'C-o-l-o-s-s-u-s' or 'B-o-i-s-t-e-r-o-u-s'.

The giants kept watching the attractive movements of the little creatures that beautified their turf.

Meanwhile, they ate slowly as they chatted. They shared jokes too, and had a great moment of laughter and also exchanged ideas. Everybody wanted to be better versions of themselves too, like in the humanistic world. '*Yakety-yak – yakety-yak*'. It was all going down well. Some were coughing in the process but, with cool water right next to them, buoyancy was kept up. It served as medication at an arm's reach. The water was put in ostrich eggshells that were attractively ornamented with beads and dyed plant seeds. The seeds queerly resembled teeth of ferocious animals. It was part of their myth to drink from these, typifying significance and dominance; and every individual had their own.

"Hey, Starwartle, why don't you wrap up some left overs into kraft paper and give to our Behemoth food master? A handsome measure of course, for a VORACIOUS ogress..."

All of a sudden, Johnny-Warlock was locomoting in his own gear – a vitriolic one! He even went closer to sit right next to Food-Killer.

"Wouldn't it make a perfect take-away for you, Food-Killer, which can serve you for the next five days or so, but *who knows?* – It might just turn out to be only a single day's helping. Or perhaps tonight's midnight snack...*ha-ha-ha-ha-ha!*' Johnny-Warlock went on... and laughed sarcastically, winking his eye at the female mammoth.

Food-Killer gaped at him in awe, grimacing. She could not believe her ears. Johnny-Warlock's words had made her day, ironically. Any special addition to her hidden gem was ostensibly manna.

Fellow monsters even went ahead and honoured the gesture.

"For sure, she's still our head cook here. Thanks for the brilliant idea Warlock, she absolutely deserves it. She has already paid her dues in honesty." Twelve-eyed, the great, chipped in – sprightly! He called Starwartle and advised her to pack a tote bagful, which Food-Killer would collect at the end of the day.

The tote bag was made of plant fibre, roughly twenty litres in capacity. The size was a tiny fraction of Food-Killer's hidden bale, but as long as she got the food as promised, that would still make a difference by being a bonus to her secret lot, waiting to be retrieved later on from the bush.

Johnny-Warlock was left dumbfounded when his gesture was well received and made official. Clearly, he had not anticipated the sharp turn of things – his act of trying to humiliate Food-Killer had ended up being a trophy instead.

"Shucks! ..." he groaned, reaching for his water. He kept the ostrich shell fixed to his mouth – frozen, for two to three minutes after having sipped up the last few drops. That gave Food-Killer a wracking belly-laugh! She went on and on, pressing her stomach hard. It took her a long time to recover before she was able to talk.

"*Who am I?*" she said. "Treated like royalty always. Even in dumbest moments, I rise like a Phoenix."

She spoke stroking her chest and, after a minute, fists were on haunches.

"I'm a 'built-in' Behemoth member – very crucial, unlike other ogres. Won't mention names..." She tattled in her well-known pompous drawl, looking straight into Monster Johnny-Warlock's eyes. "Don't try me again; you'll be left with an egg on your face," she warned.

Given the way her mouth was partying, the giantess should have pre-calculated that she could now walk away freely with her hidden treasure, given the bestowed official package.

"*Err,* Food-Killer, please! Spare us your ho-hum lectures." Jack-eyed showed up unceremoniously, disrupting the ongoing fracas. He was coming to rescue Johnny-Warlock. He had seen from afar that something had gone amiss and his friend was somewhat under attack. He did not even care to know exactly what was going on.

"Come with me, Johnny. You must pick an instrument before they all run out." King Jack-eyed pulled his buddy's hand to help him up from where he was docking.

"He's not bound with chains – he can surely do it all by himself." Without a doubt, Food-Killer was relishing in a savage bubble. She was fidgeting her legs like she was running out of time to be somewhere very important, but she was all about pecking and certainly, she persisted... "The ship almost sank before the sun was even shining, Captain Jack-eyed."

"We're smooth sailing now, so don't cripple the fiesta." Jack-eyed was brusque. Monster Johnny-Warlock rose up, keeping his eyes on Jack-eyed, shrugging off Food-Killer's cold comments.

"Oh, you mentioned instruments. Where are they? Flutes, drums and whatever...." said Warlock. The two stood there for a few minutes, chatting. "I'd been wondering where everyone else was getting them from." Johnny-Warlock's eyes livened up as he conversed with his close pal. "Yeah, certainly, percussions will be good for me; I can barely feel my feet right now." He tried to do a dance move but failed. "'Feels like I'm on stilts." He looked very puzzled.

"They surely don't look that bad at all, Warlock," said Jack-eyed, peering closely at the feet in question.

"Maybe I got pricked somewhere on my soles by some bloody poisonous spines, although I see nothing odd stuck on them," he suggested, pinching his forehead, as if he were trying to recall how the entire route, to and from, Arcane really looked like physically.

"What! Were you not wearing shoes... pounding all the way to another kingdom barefoot?" Jack-eyed was shocked, but he quickly pulled himself together, masking his irritation.

Johnny-Warlock moaned, trying to do some light warm-up kicks. He stopped before achieving anything meaningful. "I don't know anymore... look, they were itchy earlier on, then came pulsating pains, and now they've just gone numb... I wonder what the next minute holds for-"

"Stop, stop, hey, you'll surely be okay." Jack-eyed tried to cut him short before he further frustrated himself.

"I don't see myself throwing any moves tonight," he still groaned, clutching his legs, gazing concernedly at the discomforting feet. His eyes were bloodshot. He generally looked very weary.

"I can help you sculpt another pair of feet. There's plentiful good clay around here, no voyaging needed..." the talky ogress hatched a ludicrous plan; and no one else other than Food-Killer would taunt to such magnitude. "Just letting you know there's a willing volunteer here." She kept banging on.

"For real – if I were you, Food-Killer, I'd be laying low now... very, very low," Johnny-Warlock countered with a blurred warning, but the female mammoth showed no care.

"You're lucky, though Warlock, smooth-spoken like this whilst in pain... Avid-Thwack's brains went crackers after zonking out."

"Whoa, enough Food-Killer." Jack-eyed raised his index finger to silence her. He turned to Warlock and winged his arm over his shoulder. "Relax... I know you – always up to getting really down. It's Boisterous after all, who wouldn't?" He switched to dabbing his back, "In thirty minutes you'll be frolicking. The gods are listening too; you just got to believe. Forget all the spoken ill, please." He articulated this in a very soothing, silvery voice. "We might also have to fuse a concoction to douse the feet, perhaps. It's a great tincture. I mean... nature heals, just in case it's indeed some grievous thorns that invaded your system."

Food-Killer could not hold up for even a bit – she never stopped rolling...

Johnny completely discounted her, tilting his body forward and clicking his fingers in response to Jack-eyed's sincere concern. He transitioned to rocking his shoulders in the split of a second – making his elbows flair out rhythmically, matching the sound of instruments that was emanating from another end. His legs were just static.

"Or rather drop a crawling dance, the Monster-Jumbo style, and save your throbbing feet," Food-Killer proposed, scoffing.

"Cheerio, Head Cook. Want see you do your thing in the arena. Don't just be a master of obnoxiousness and hopefully your stomach gives you the chance." Johnny-Warlock had to deliver a final statement that would be of vengeance before walking away.

"A lifetime laurel for bickering is certainly due to her," King Jack-eyed lampooned further and laughed light-heartedly, to make his words befit a joke.

"Let's whoop it up, cronies!" Food-Killer called out behind their backs, in a foghorn loud voice. She did not mind at all. Whatever had been mentioned, she seemed very relieved – having cited all her feelings earlier. She was all lively, bathing in a euphoric phase.

# 17

The party was continuing regardless – all fireworks. Every other monster looked ecstatic. The sun was almost turning golden-orange and the weather was very cool, perfectly conducive to heighten any excitement. All instruments had been pulled out and members who wanted to participate were already playing their favourite. There were a few drums, and Monster-Jumbo led the crew in setting the rhythm. Most females were clasping gourd shakers and tambourines. It was not surprising that the Colossus king chose to be a part of this elating group. He loved associating with ogresses. The female giants also constituted a larger voting population than their male counterparts.

The only weakness Jack-eyed had was drinking himself to a stooge, but he knew when to pull out his cunning trait to cover up the fault.

Marimbas had to be there too – an integral part of their sanctification – together with trumpets and flutes. Flutes and guitars were only played by a few select individuals. All other monsters sang their lungs out as they benignly celebrated together. Seventh heaven, it was – marvellous and hearty! They were all in high spirits. Monster-Monsleek was exultantly delighted, playing her favourite instrument, the flute. She danced softly... snake charmer moves.

With gourd shakers in all six hands, the monster-king Jack-eyed shook them like there was never a 'next time' to ever feature again.

On the other side was Fiery-Fireball, playing a guitar. He leaped backwards and forward and sideways – left and right – but gently, as if he trampled on hot charcoal. His shoulder blades were popping out through his vest at intervals, in unison with his motion. He had been transferred to a whole different world seemingly, where love and peace exclusively manifested. His hair had been left disarranged in the process; with every strand freely interpreting the art of dancing and the sound of instruments in their own unique ways – bouncing, or simply sprung vertically upright. Other strands were tipping forward, backwards and sideways, in line with the cadence of his legs. Other filaments had, however, just gone limp – succumbing to the dampness of sweat on his head.

His spirit kept him going; observing Boisterous with dynamism, and surely his fingers didn't come short either – strumming the strings of the guitar with unmatchable high proficiency. The vest had been the best choice of garment for him, meeting up with all his demands – both somatic and spiritual. The fiery energy left many ogresses possessed by exuberant fits of excitement. They fanatically flapped their hands in the air, honouring the giant, Fiery-Fireball.

Monster Johnny-Warlock lingered on. He just sat there in the crowd, swaying his head to the melody – if only he had a spare stick to clean his ears... His feet were swollen still, but slightly subsided. Food-Killer's chase had done him no favours. It had been worsened by the long race that had subsequently followed. He had not found lighter percussions to play, unfortunately. All the instruments were gone by the time he went to check, together with Jack-eyed.

In spite of the mishaps, all the anxiety and tension from earlier conflicts seemed to have dissipated. Warlock was certainly in sync with the hubbub – juddering his upper body and the head!

Dancing only with her forefingers was Food-Killer. Her wrists were now tinselled with jewellery, which jingled subtly. Leaning against the wall by the hall entrance, the monster head cook was getting carried away. Her tail also jiggled to the jubilation. The rest of her body, however, did not exhibit any willingness to shake at any point in time. It only ended with fingers and the cauda.

Her ears were only taking in the marimba sounds. It was her preferred contrivance. The marimba players thumped the wooden bars with monster-made mallets as if possessed. Dancing her forefingers still, Monster Food-Killer's eyes got glued onto the restless mallets!

Such ambience! In the open air, all the monsters were zappy, on top of the world. Seven cauldrons with steamy pumpkins were brought to them. Replenishing energy along the way was a necessity, and most of them favoured the warty goblin, which had been spiced up with plenty of cinnamon powder, and the spice strongly effused! The pots that had the crookneck squashes were touched last, but still served their purpose.

The giants became uproarious and broke into their famous tune!

*Monster fear, Monster fear....*
*We rule the world with Monster fear.......*
*We conquer the world with Monster terror....*
*Monster fear, Monster fear....*
*Who is the hector of predators?*
*In my face tell me now...*
*Victorious hector of predators*
*Monster fear, Monster fear....*

It did not take long before Monster Johnny-Warlock found himself in the arena. All pain and swelling seemed to have magically vanished. He danced effortlessly, unveiling his new skills – unpacking each and every technique expressively. He swayed his body, like he was soaring amidst a kettle of condors. He could do it all night – enchanting the ogres who sat clapping steadfast in the audience. All eyes were affixed on him for close to an hour of his zestful act.

"You're back from the dead, Warlock!" Food-Killer called out in a loud, grating voice before crumbling into a fit of laughter. Johnny looked up. They made eye contact, and he simply waved at her as he proudly walked over, going to join in, into the circle of participants who were getting ready to perform a Colossus sequential dance routine, which was officially known as the *Colondor dance.*

The dance held a profound magnitude in their beliefs. The significance lay in the opening of arms, the rotation and revolution moves, and the quivering of flared out fingers, which represented the Condor when it's about to take off – outstretching its wings and soaring into the skies!

They stepped magnificently, going in harmony with their Boisterous tune, and the Teras guests who were not well acquainted with the dance routine had to quickly learn, to join in the fun and also extend solidarity to their hosts.

"Here, here, I'll explain to you!" In haste, Monster Fiery-Fireball volunteered to coach them. He was entirely agog, "It's easy," he said. "Nothing can ever be difficult for monsters. Come on and reveal yourselves if you really are…" he continued.

Everyone rippled! In a few seconds, a circle for learners took shape.

"This is how it goes. First, we hold each other's shoulders. Do a kick with the left leg – six times. Move, going around clockwise six steps too – maintaining narrow paces. Now stop. Take a lunge position, individually, crook your arms to the front... then flare out your fingers with palms facing you; quiver the hands. Hold it there – then, quivering your hands in the lunge position do a clockwise rotation. Clap and jump! Hold shoulders again. Do the kick; now with the right leg – six times and follow the same as we did initially with the left leg."

They followed.

"You're all doing great! Yeah, let's keep at it... 1-2-3, let's go..." The husky voice of Monster Fiery-Fireball rocketed from the learners' circle, transcending the ogres who were singing. He made it very fascinating for the beginners, and the crew performed pretty well.

On and on the dance routine went, repeatedly – and the circle continued growing larger and more sizzling... The senior pros integrated themselves into the circle too, and it was a colossal evening!

# 18

Off the beaten track, a cloud of bats went into a frenzy, fluttering their membranous wings around in the hall... bothering the ogres who were busy on the dance floor. The creatures were now on the hunt down for something to bite. It was a natural clock to everyone, all the same... ringing bells that night-time had just fallen.

According to their tradition in Colossus, this was also the outright slot for them to do their sacrifices to their gods, asking for protection and abundance. For those with transgressions, it was the rightful moment to plead for forgiveness and leave Behemoth restored and complete and begin the new year with a clean slate. The operation was open to everyone, including guests.

It was pretty much three quarters of the present population that went into the queue for the cleansing observance. Food-Killer was there and Monster-Monsleek too, amongst the much larger number constituting the Colossus fraction. Only a few heads amidst the crowd belonged to Teras.

Food-Killer was getting too busy, without even fall of four minutes. Neglecting to focus on herself – her eyes were constantly leering at Monster-Starwartle, who was fourteen ogres ahead of her. Starwartle had completely shut her dorsal eyes, concentrating on the benediction hour.

It's very likely that Food-Killer was ruminating... processing what kind of sin on Colossus land Starwartle had committed. She perpetuated with her scanning conduct as if there was something written on the back of Starwartle's head. Her blinkers skittered past those who were standing closest to her, like Monster Ghost-Hound – or rather they plausibly deserved to be there. Johnny-Warlock could clearly see everything that was happening in the hall, but he showed no reaction. He stood wholly solemn towards the end of the waiting line. Right at the end was Monster Fiery-Fireball, only four heads from Johnny-Warlock.

As soon as the damsel got ushered into the sanctified room, at her turn, Monster Food-Killer could not keep her lips closed. "*Upon my word*, the quiet... so called subservient ones, can be the most devious. What is Starwartle doing here? Perhaps the Acardia mountains could have answers for us." Rubbing her nose with her forefinger, she dished out her feeble thoughts to the monsters who were around her. They simply hissed back, showing no interest in engaging in the conversation.

Later on, after the benediction hour, Monster Freaky-Buddy, together with Twelve-eyed and King Jack-eyed, officially congratulated and crowned Monster Fiery-Fireball as the champion runner of the year. The crowing segment happened outside under a delightful moonlight. "Fiery... Fiery! Fiery-Fireball!" the boastful monster shouted as he trudged back into the crowd after being crowned. He was honoured with the Revolving Colossus Accolade.

He took out pellet bolides from his pouch; a lot of them this time around. It brought about immediate caterwauling. His folks were cringing and complaining, but their voices were all muffled, surprisingly. Fiery boisterously hurled the pellets into air, using the special pipe, and they propelled farther away from the congregation. Jack-eyed and Twelve-eyed just looked on. They were probably relieved that it was happening in the wild, far away from any innocent ogre.

"Fiery... Fiery! Fiery-Fireball," he cranked up his voice proclaiming his name as the pellets burst from their shells with a soft detonating sound. They sparked one after the other, producing numerous magnificent stars that mushroomed in style – right there in the air – before dying out. Every monster rose up to the phenomena. The sparkles were soft and very bright, and they looked very beautiful in the late evening hour. They glinted, as they moved simultaneously in awesome patterns. Only this time around, the whole monster crowd roared, applauding. They found it very fascinating – the attractiveness of it, and the seraphic feel.

"Won't you do this again at our next celebration, Fiery-Fireball?" King Jack-eyed suggested, misty eyed.

"My win or loss... I'll forever do it; every Boisterous," it did not take seconds before Fiery acknowledged. He placed his tools on the ground at once and gave a sincere bow.

"Soon it'll be *de rigueur,* Fiery-Fireball, you said so – all our fiestas..." said the Colossus kingpin. He was overwhelmed, just like every other attendee. He gathered himself and continued, "See, it's surpassingly splendiferous when done in the open like this, and not against kinfolks... We should have known sooner." His voice was modulated.

"Like our condor – fearless we unfurl and soar!" they all crooned in unison, with absolute pride. It was an awe-inspiring occasion for the giants.

Monster-Monsleek screamed afterwards that Fiery-Fireball should make an oath not to ever use his pellets on any one of them ever again, which other ogres agreed with. They could not have waited for yet another time or chance that lay somewhere in the future to mention it. Many of them had had a smack of the little pellets before!

Various awards were then extended too, to many. They were all wrapped in pure jubilation and were grateful. They had their own special kind of accolades, as ogres – odd and distinct from the norm of gold, silver and bronze for ordinary people, in the human world. Theirs were made out of clay, with majestic patterns impressed on them. Every streak had its own cultural meaning to it.

The award for the most popular ogress – an attendees' choice – went to the giantess in the ash-grey choker dress.

The votes favoured her, taking over from the previous winner, Monster-Monsleek.

Teaser-Macabre was the winning ogress's name!

The crown accentuated her costume, and she never got a chance to rest her feet after the win. It was her moment. She strolled beautifully everywhere, in all directions – parading her fresh look of high couture and thanking the voters. The grisly ribbons on the train of her dress were now lively as they swayed along with her charismatic movements... very enticingly, akin to snakes that have been swept over in a drive to tantalizing their prey. Any other mind would anticipate the ghoulish pieces of fabric to flick out slobbery forked tongues at any moment. One would only be left to imagine what tongue colours were to spring forth – blue, green, cream, purple, black or the beetroot red; tears of the Draco Tree!

Fellow mammoths praised her name in soft tones, but yet with great enthusiasm.

*'Colossus Queen, Teaser-Macabre...'*

*'Teaser-Macabre, Colossus Queen...'*

Teaser-Macabre grew even taller with pride, and so it seemed did her fingernails. She invisibly poked a few tender hearts, especially that of Monster-Monsleek.

Monsleek was sitting with a group of rowdy males. She seemed disconnected by what was happening around her. Her soul was probably pining for the title that had just fallen off, but she had had her time – and considering all that had transpired throughout the day, it would have been unbelievable should she have won. Her lips were mouthing completely different syllables from 'T e a s e r - M a c a b r e' like almost everyone else was doing. It looked as though she murmured 'H o w   c o m e... h o w   c o m e...' repeatedly.

"Monsleek, Monsleek!" Avid-Thwack called her, but there was no answer. She screamed louder three more times and still...

Monsleek could get away with it, blaming the rowdy group she was sitting with, but the screams of her name were goring to an eardrum.

"Are you alright, Monsleek?" asked Avid-Thwack. She had finally walked up to her and gazed at her, right in her face.

"*Oh, Avid...*"

Monsleek rose up for a hug – a lengthy one – and she never said much. The warmth of her body most likely reported, crying out everything to her dear friend in silence – all that was roiling her mind and choking her voice.

The hug left her with etchings of Thwack's teeth on the side of her neck. The markings could be pardoned this time around, when flicking back the pages of Colossus chronicles.

Celebratory proceedings had to go ahead! Boisterous Day was still unravelling, although it was narrowing closer to the end.

All monsters were then summoned to go back into the hall, and they did.

# 19

As the vote counting began, a flurry of movement also arose. Some monsters started leaving the hall haphazardly; with others returning momentarily and a couple of other groups stretching much longer. The same faces that were in the queue for the important cleansing procedure constituted the larger number of the ogres who were leaving, one after the other. They all meandered in different directions, going to retrieve their hidden food packs.

Food-Killer had got carried away with her endless chattering. By the time she got to the bush, she found a good number of mammoths creeping out of there, hoisting their loads. She ran to her spot, panic stricken!

She got there in no time, but her bag was gone! She looked around, just for the sake of it, but it was gone. The giantess was sullen when she observed spills of what looked like ice-cream. The grass was wet and matted down on that particular area where the bale had been sitting. The sweet desert had surely oozed from the package. She knelt and dabbed the area with her fingers – rubbed them together and finally licked, just to verify.

"My food is gone, folks!" the female mammoth screamed in a foghorn tone. "The bale was sitting right here! It's gone – vaporized, folks!" Her hands rose up slowly to the back of her head.

Nobody seemed to care.

*Who would have wanted to reveal their faces in that instant, instead of rejoicing over the free gift of darkness that was upon them – gallantly enshrouding their ongoing mischief?*

They were all busy trying to move their own loot before getting caught by any figures of high authority. Only owls that were roosting high up in the trees paid attention to her... by merely gazing spookily.

Everything meant nothing to Food-Killer. She wanted her bale back!

She was shocked when she caught sight of other packages that were still scattered around there, within her territory; all of them appearing intact. There were four, including the one she had secretly opened and rebuked. She appeared dizzy. Instincts of denial scintillated all over her body, although the state of affairs was undeniable. The giantess eventually closed her eyes tight – very tight – creasing up her entire face. She held the stance for a reasonable amount of time, before flicking her eye-lids open.

Food-Killer realised her situation was real.

"'Got your bickering honour, right?" a familiar voice blurted from behind her. She almost fell on her knees. It had come like a gravity bomb dropped right onto the middle of her head.

"J-Warlock, how could you? How could you?" In her state of dizziness, she managed to project her voice. "Where the hell did you put my bag?" the giantess groaned. Indeed she wanted her food items back.

Monster Johnny-Warlock exploded into demoniac laughter, inflicting more pain on her languishing soul. "Let's see who's feeding on pasture tonight," he went on to say.

"What are you even gushing about? I hate you!" Food-Killer was bewildered. She just stood there, shrieking in the dark, trying to come to terms with what was occurring. The moment she turned around again, after the miserable encounter, the few bags that were hidden in the vicinity were all gone. They had been collected gradually while she was not paying attention.

Her situation worsened. She behaved as if she had just tumbled onto a bed of pins and needles as her body quivered. Emotional distress hampered her reasoning capacity, pretty much as time did. Chances were now limited to almost zero, for her to come up with any tangible fall-back plans.

"I could have at least made a healthy salad with the greens and yellows... Oh, I wish–" she yearned out to the universe, with her cheeks soaking up with tears, as she spotted a couple of monsters straggling from different directions, walking out of the bush, carrying their own loot. As plain as pikestaff, she had thought of stealing other monsters' treasures too, but it was out of the question now! The bush had been cleared.

"*Bwahaha!!*" Johnny-Warlock could not contain displaying how charged up he was at having outfoxed the Colossus food master.

"Now, that's a genuine medal you've just won..." he pronounced to Food-Killer, but she appeared not to have fully registered what he was actually saying. Warlock did not stay there any longer, for a probable further conversation – yabbering the night away.

Briefly afterward, the giant dashed out of the woods.

Alas – Food-Killer was right behind, scooting!

"You'd better rush back to Behemoth and get your official pack before it vanishes too. Running after me... hovering will surely reward you with nothing," he warned Food-Killer, who was looking roused up enough to embark on what she knew best – avenging.

Food-Killer was extremely disappointed. There was pain in her step. Her poor feet had to endure conveying her knackered body back to Behemoth...

It was just then, as soon as she finally made it, dragging into the hall, when the name of the new king was being announced and formally presented.

*Ayes always have it* – Monster Jack-eyed had made it again! Fourth time in a row! It stirred unmatchable boisterous bliss in the huge crowd but all mattered nix to Food-Killer. She was bent out of shape and her senses were ostensibly absent. A large group of delirious ogres was now assembling for yet another round of the 'Colondor dance'.

"Like our condor – fearless we unfurl and soar!" they chanted.

Food-Killer tossed her cloak onto the floor and walked tardily past.

In the passageway was Monster-Pinniped, planning with Jumbo, the Teras ogre, that he feel free to consider being his family's guest for the night. He also wanted him to join in for an evening swim at Terror Ditch, after the Boisterous Day proceedings, which were winding down. Jumbo's reactions to the idea punctuated an episode of a dream come true situation. However, the two quickly paused... having to veer way for Food-Killer, who seemed to be walking blindfolded. They looked at her strangely as she talked to herself as she clomped past them.

"Johnny-Warlock has scalded my feelings really... slashing my Boisterous plans with his evil sickle..." Food-Killer grizzled all the way to the kitchen door to pick up her parcel and perhaps any other leftovers. But, in a moment, she was goggle-eyed, finding herself faced with rolled over drums, all empty. The heavy ancient wooden door was wide open, amplifying the degree of the insult. There was no way her food parcel could have been spared; it was crystal clear.

"He was lurking around after me," she complained further in a throaty tone, and her anger was elevating. "He is the Croc–" she reflected, breathing heavily and rested her upper body on the table.

"*So, what* – he was laying *au naturel* up there in a tree? *Sick...* cruel trick of fate!"

She bunched up her fingers into a fist, but frail, with her face buried in the crook of the other arm. The rustic kitchen table was translated into a crying shoulder.

*Hey! I'm the invisible alien. I couldn't stay much longer to see the monsters walk off after the festival – sorry. Monster Ghost-Hound was beginning to sense my presence – he is nocturnal!*

**~~~ THE END ~~~**

# EPILOGUE

## KEY SIGNATURE DISH

### (i)

That
Distinctive dessert bowl,
Freshly made Mixed Fruit Salad
By All-time Cordon Bleu exhorts
Deciphering world,
And what belongs...
Surpassing it is
Great but delicate!
Supposing
Pollutant sin and
Phantoms, so like
Pathogens and allies,
Vanish or ash – eroding to seas;
The surpassing exhibited dish,
Well intact as delivered would last!
And the great piece of art-work
So as its value,
Up to heritage,
Would be ever cherished
And lasting as

Afterlife...
(ii)


The once empty Fruit Salad bowl,
A prior plain world,
Only earned value then...
When exceptionally enriched and embellished
With carefully picked assorted fruits;
Well proportioned,
And passionately layered to complement purpose,
And unbridle sole artistry of its maker.
Variant colours of fruits unify,
In the same space of bowl,
Creating such estimable chatoyance
They entwine their nutrients –
And chorus 'nourish-theme' phrase
As one –
Esprit de corps!
Their varying unique flavours cordially mingle
backing each other...
Different shapes and textures –
With no fuss, complement.
Lavished with dressing and signature spices,
And ornamented with garnish,
Cordon Bleu... and the bowl as a whole,
Yields Magic –
Ambrosial Mixed Fruit Dessert!

It means World...
Culling out a fraction or such
Of the exceptionally exhibited dish,
Mutates;
It tarnishes just but the whole bowl,
All belong...
Cordon Bleu exclusively holds the key!
He decides on Array and arrays himself
He calculates when to let off or replenish
He controls quanta of his dish,
Exhibition after exhibition.
Very artistic in cuisine he is
What he sees and feels of his creation -
...Majestic...
...All is meant...
He holds the highest title
Ancient folding another,
On Array is supreme key signature dish,
It's the World!
A creation by
God

*Auxie Mzil-Lehang*